Merry Ct
from
 xxxx

Robert Green

Jack Jones

authorHOUSE

AuthorHouse™ *UK Ltd.*
500 Avebury Boulevard
Central Milton Keynes, MK9 2BE
www.authorhouse.co.uk
Phone: 08001974150

© 2009, 2011 Jack Jones. All rights reserved.

No part of this book may be reproduced, stored in a retrieval system, or transmitted by any means without the written permission of the author.

First published by AuthorHouse 09/13/2011

ISBN: 978-1-4389-3536-2 (sc)

Printed in the United States of America
Bloomington, Indiana

This book is printed on acid-free paper.

Chapter 1

"Robert can you bring the Rover round please?"

"Yes, Philip."

The Rover spoke volumes about its owner, A 3-Litre P5 MkIII Coupe, grey bodywork with red leather upholstery and Wilton carpets. They both stated class and purpose, without having to shout from the rooftops, look at me. Also that Philip addressed Robert by his Christian name belied his status in society. As Robert approached the house he could see Phillip, impeccable as usual, dark blue sweater, white shirt & tie, black slacks and shoes polished to a mirror where if he were that type of man could check that his bushy hair was behaving itself, making his way down the steps, as he came to a halt Phillip reached the last step, crossed over to the car and climbed in.

"Synchronicity, not bad." Philip said, as he sat in the passenger seat.

Robert replied "Certainly makes life easier, you did not mention anything yesterday so where are we going?"

An embarrassed Philip said, "Sorry, should have said something, into the village. I had a call from the local bookstore, a book I have been waiting for is in, it has been quite a while coming and had forgotten about it."

Robert noted the forgetfulness and Philip's disquiet at his lapse in memory.

Chapter 2

In the few short months that Robert had been in Philips employment synchronicity was a pretty good word. He just seemed to fit with Phillip, Victoria (his wife), Elizabeth (his daughter) the household and anything else that came under Philips domain. He had yet to meet Thomas, the son.

To the casual observer Philip and Robert were miles apart. Philip was wealthy, ex army and at 64 years of age still walked with an upright gait ready to stand to attention. Lord Hawthorn was Philip's correct title and that was how most people addressed him. Not because he expected it and not because people felt it was the right thing to do. It was his presence, a kind family man who would do his utmost to help any one, people respected him.

Robert on the other hand was ex SAS and also had presence a menacing presence. His last military duty had only been two years since, but now it seemed a lifetime ago and on a different planet. He had joined the Army in 1986, straight from school and loved it. Discipline and routine. It gave him a sense of purpose. After three years as an infantryman he was asked if he would like to go on a course. He hadn't turned down a challenge up till then, so off he went. Robert craved army life but this was different. The SAS. Each challenge presented, became a personal battle sleet, snow, wind and rain did not deter Robert. If anything, the obstructions drove him on, to do it better and to do it faster. At the end of the training course there were only two men left. Robert Green and Jim Coldershot. They became lifetime friends knowing that they could trust each other implicitly.

Because, of a severe knee injury Jim was retired out of the army. In his own words "I can't serve as half a man." Coldershot joined the police force and was making quite a name for himself. There is only so much you could do from behind a desk and Jim was regularly to be found on the front line of operations dodgy knee or not.

Robert's career in the SAS went from strength to strength. He held all key appointments, the youngest

RSM, Regiment Sergeant Major, in the history of the SAS and was reportedly in line for a Captains badge. That was until he went to Iraq early 2003. Robert was used to men moaning about their lot, not supplied with adequate kit, arms not correct for the job they had to do, the promise of new and updated artillery was not being fulfilled. He had learnt to do the best with what you are given. But this was fellow SAS men moaning, the disquiet stemmed not from the lack of equipmanet, but what were they doing there. Robert had to agree. This was not their war.

April 2004 3 a.m. on patrol one morning Robert and three other young soldiers were in a supposedly safe area of Basra when they were ambushed. One of his men fell to the ground, dead. Robert signalled for the other two, Greaves and Marshall to join him. They moved slowly and quietly behind fallen walls when a bullet whistled past Robert's head. He had pinpointed the sniper hiding in an old disused van, firing out of the slightly open back doors. The only problem they had was getting close enough to the van to eliminate their assailant. From their experience the sniper was sure to be a suicide bomber. Robert studied the two young soldiers and told them to cover him.

When Robert was level with the van, approximately 200 foot between him and the target he turned to make sure the two young soldiers were in position and ready. Ideally he would have sent one of the men around the other side so that they could have attacked on three fronts but they were too inexperienced. Just as he was about to give the signal someone opened fire on them, Robert took a bullet to the shoulder. Greaves returned fire and got a hit, Robert signalled to open fire on the van. As expected the van exploded. Their luck was in, they retreated and made it back to barracks, one dead one wounded. Robert thanked Greaves before he was taken into surgery.

Lying in his hospital bed Blackstock head of operations came to see him. Fully expecting Robert to be apologetic, subservient and keen to get back into action he was somewhat taken aback by the SAS man lying in the bed. Robert told him in no uncertain terms that he was a highly trained SAS operative and he did not expect to be sent out on patrol and more to the point with kids.

Blackstock argued that "One of the kids saved his life".

Robert countered, "One of those kids was meant to have checked that van."

Over the next few days several officers came to see Robert but he could not be dissuaded. This was not the army he had joined it was now run on cutbacks and involved in battles they had no right to be fighting. He had fought in far more ferocious battles than this latest skirmish and had always come out on top but when the intelligence is wrong, the men inexperienced and fighting against local insurgents you're on to a hiding to nothing.

Because of his wound he would leave the service with a full pension. But he would leave with a black mark against his name and that hurt.

So here we was in the employment of the Hawthorns, and admitted to himself he was rather enjoying it. Philip was a true gent. **Both men had much in common. They had faced the harsh realities of war, came close to death and witnessed the slaughter of innocent civilians. Those experiences took root in your soul and ran though the blood that pumped the heart and fed the mind. It would have been impossible to come away from those experiences unchanged, Robert and Phillip silently understood this.**

Chapter 3

As they approached the village Robert said

"Its market day" he continued. "shall I park up by the Church?"

"Yes" Philip replied. Still bothered by his failing memory.

The car settled by the old church wall, the two men walked down the small hill towards the village centre. But because of the throng of people, many of whom passed pleasantries with Lord Hawthorn and many of the women tried to catch Robert's eye, it took some time to reach their destination. Once there the business transaction was quickly dealt with. Philip said, "Fancy drink?"

"I will have a cup of tea." replied Robert.

As they made their way to the "Badger," a public house Robert noticed up ahead a young woman struggling with a pushchair trying to make her way. Three youths approached the woman from behind Robert sensing danger, quickened his pace. He arrived just as the youths barged past the woman, she started to fall towards the road. Robert, with one hand on the pushchair leant forward and grabbed the woman by her coat lapels pulling her out of the way of an oncoming bus. The youths carried on oblivious, Philip arrived and immediately took charge. Robert's eyes never left the youths and once Philip and the woman were safely ensconced in the Badger, he was in pursuit.

Robert could see the three youths ahead still barging past people, eager to get somewhere. They turned right off the main high street into a quiet alley and so did Robert. Abruptly they came to a halt and crouched down. Only then did one of the youths notice Robert. Hastily, shoving something into their pockets, they stood up. Having already assessed their potential, first when walking towards them and then walking away from them Robert knew that this bunch of kids who just needed a scare, it was a far from dangerous situation. Now facing them he was certain, especially when two of the cretins shuffled behind the spokesman. Who, with everything he could muster said, "Who the fuck are you?"

Robert thought to himself, even in a pathetic bunch of individuals like this there was a fucking leader. Robert moved to within a few feet and asked them to empty their pockets and drop the contents to the floor. The two cretins behind the spokesman duly obliged. Robert staring at the leader moved to within breathing distance of this sorry kid, as young as he was he understood that only pain and misery lay in the stranger's eyes. Robert emptied his pockets for him and said "In your eagerness to divvy out the drugs you knocked a woman into the road, she was lucky she didn't get hit by a bus and so were you." With that Robert ground the packets into the floor backed out of the alley and made his way to the Badger.

Robert found Phillip and the woman sitting at a table. She had a cup of tea, Philip poured one for Robert from the pot standing on the table. Robert noticed the almost indiscernible shake while Philip was handling the pot. Philip made the introductions, Robert this is Honey and her son Michael, Honey this is Robert.

Robert said to Honey "Not a good day for coming

into the village."

Honey replied "I wouldn't normally, it's just that Michael is not too well, took him to the doctors and was on my way to the chemist."

Philip said to Robert "would you mind."

Robert said to Honey as long as you don't mind I can get the medicine for you. Honey willingly handed over the prescription to Robert. By the time Robert got back to the pub a taxi had been ordered to take Honey and Michael home. Robert collapsed the pushchair and stowed it away in the boot of the taxi, Philip handed some money over to Honey and spoke to the taxi driver. As the taxi pulled away she wound the window down and shouted God bless you both.

Robert quickly slipped back into the pub and collected the book that Philip had purchased earlier. He handed it over to a sheepish looking Philip.

Chapter 4

Later that day Robert came up to the house, Hawthorn Hall built between 1755 and 1765 a classic Palladian style home set in 950 acres of parks and farmland. Much to Philip's and later Victoria's, credit the house and the lands that surrounded it lacked any austere intimidation. In Philip's family for generations the house came with responsibility. Naturally Philip realised all that was expected of him and did all that was necessary and more to maintain and improve the building and the land. Of course the dwelling was much too big for the family that now occupied it.

Robert sought out Victoria and asked if he could speak to her in private. He asked if she had noticed anything different about Philip. She stood with her head bowed leaning back against the window that faced south out of the drawing-room, the backdrop constantly changing as clouds raced across the sky. When she looked up directly at Robert he could see the tears that filled her eyes. Victoria said "Of course. After 25 years of living with the same man you can not help but notice" she added "a friend of ours who happens to be a neurological consultant is visiting next Wednesday."

"Philip ever the pragmatist will undergo whatever is necessary to find out what the problem is. In his own words better to know who's buggering about with you than taking it up the arse unawares." Robert smiled. Victoria carried on "Only guesswork at the moment but Parkinsons or Alzheimers spring to mind."

Robert had only heard of these diseases and not encountered them but as Victoria had said it was only guesswork, best wait for a proper diagnosis. Robert uttered, "Probably a pointless question but is there anything I can do to help?"

"Robert" Victoria said "are you completely oblivious to all that you do for this family and staff? Since you arrived here everything has changed. You would have expected that the arrival of a younger and fitter man would have put the cat amongst the pigeons but somehow you managed not to do that. Your very presence has been a fillip to the household. Dare I say no, no I will leave it at that. Suffice to say do not you fucking leave us."

Robert had never heard Victoria swear and was taken aback. He said "Where is Philip now?"

Victoria, gazing at Robert said, "He is on the quad bike taking the dogs for a run."

Robert replied, "Ok, I'll catch up with him."

He knew Philip's routine and made for the lower field. As he walked along he thought about Victoria and what she had said. Which wasn't easy, because to think about anything Victoria said meant you had to think about Victoria. She was stunning; he had never encountered a woman like her. Truly a gift from the Gods. Hazel eyes, lush mouth, golden coloured hair that fell onto her shoulders, five foot eight and a figure that Marilyn Monroe would have felt envious of. Aesthetically she was as near to perfect as could be. As a person she was kind generous and from what he could tell a wonderful mother and a loving wife.

Robert could not guess her age, all his guesses made

her too young to have a 20-year-old daughter and a 22-year-old son. Robert had heard of this job through his friend and had been warned to try and not fall in love with Philip's wife. Robert had dismissed that thought out of hand. For gods sake he was a 36-year-old man not a 16-year-old virgin.

The outburst, surely it had to do with Philips illness, assumed illness and what she dare not say.

Robert heard the quad and could see the dogs. He bent down ready to greet the two chocolate brown Labradors. Toby and Murphy reached him first, bounced around him for a few moments and then heard the gong, sat down, tails wagging and waited for Philip. As soon as the quad caught them up Philip released the dogs, he did not believe in holding them unnecessarily. Squire the Alsatian stood beside the quad, Philip said to the dog "You can go as well."

There was little chance of that even if the gong had sounded for dinner he would not leave his master's side.

Philip said "What brings you down here?" He carried on, "Joining us for dinner?"

Robert thought quickly "No, I was just on my way to see Alan about the Rover, heard the quad, veered off and here I am."

Philip spoke "Bollocks, you have had a word with Victoria, concluded that I need keeping an eye on and here you are. Do not lie to me. I very much appreciate the concern, in fact I would like to see you, Victoria and Elizabeth later this evening."

Robert knew an order when he heard one, even when it sounded like a request. At 9:15 p.m. Robert entered the house via the kitchen where the staff had just finished for the day. Dinner had been cleared away and the breakfast dishes were ready for the next morning. It was an extremely well run house as was the kitchen, garden and any thing else under Philip's tenure. Robert had learned very quickly that not only was this a well run establishment but the staff were happy too, and to preserve this climate Robert harmonized. Passing through the kitchen Robert took the time to enquire after people and wish them a good evening. If truth were known Robert rather enjoyed this newfound side to his character, the Philip effect, or was it the Victoria effect? He made his way out of the kitchen along the hall and knocked on the drawing-room door before entering. Inside he found

Philip, Victoria and Elizabeth.

Elizabeth now stood where Victoria had stood earlier, a beautiful young woman who would one day maybe match her mother. She was laughing at something Philip had said, Victoria put down the book she was reading and joined in with the laughter. He was greeted with a chorus of hellos from Victoria and Elizabeth; Philip stood up and offered him a drink, which he accepted. Philip also offered a drink to Victoria and Elizabeth, Victoria indicated that she still had wine in her glass and Elizabeth declined the offer. He poured a whisky each for himself and Robert.

Elizabeth sat next to her mother, the book put away. Robert sat in the beautiful old leather chair close to the hearth; the burning fire reflected its warmth in the faces of those who now sat within its proximity.

The former S.A.S man thought to himself, this was actually a very comfortable room. Dark browns and creams. Solid furniture lent the notion of antiquity but assembled in a very modern style, definitely Victoria's influence.

The lure of looking at Victoria was sometimes

difficult, however Robert had the ability to stand outside of the situation and look back in, he knew of all the inherent dangers. Of course it takes two to tango and Victoria was above all of that nonsense, furthermore even if the situation became a potential reality, he had too much respect for Philip.

Philip began with an astonishing confession. He explained "This is not the first time I have had this type of problem I just managed to keep it under wraps before."

Victoria prompted, "What was it and more importantly when?"

Philip informed them "I lost the vision in my left eye for approximately a week. That was before I met you so there is no need to blame yourself for not noticing. I am older now and thank God wiser, there has to be some benefits for old age. I know that you are all worried and so am I. I do not want to become a burden, who does? But if that is to be the scenario then better to be ready and prepared."

Victoria interrupted once again "Philip, do you think you are getting a little ahead of yourself?"

Philip "No, I just think it wiser that people are prepared, I do not want the fact that I am possibly ill going any further than this room. I know I can trust the three of you and expect your help."

Elizabeth said "What about Thomas?"

Philip angrily said, "He will turn up as soon as there is news of my impending demise."

Robert, more to quell the rising tide of resentment interjected quickly "You have my full support, for as long as you need it." Philip thanked him. With that the two men headed for the library where they would down a few more scotches and discuss all manner of things. The two women stayed in the drawing-room and discussed the animosity that existed between Philip and Thomas. Victoria knew full well the problems that Thomas had caused Philip, herself and Elizabeth. Indeed they had not seen Thomas since the summer before, he had decided to skip Christmas. A girl, perhaps a girlfriend, had had the courtesy to call them with the news that Thomas was actually going to be away for the holiday period.

For the next few days life continued as normal. Their consultant friend, a Dr Kneebone, came, asked Philip a multitude of questions spoke at length with Philip and Victoria and at the end of it suggested an MRI scan. The scan would take place in a London hospital so Victoria and Philip would make a couple of days of it. They decided to drive down the night before the scan, meet with a couple of old friends, see a show and eat out in London. The next day they would just wander, walk along the river, visit the Eye and a couple of museums. Just like a couple of young lovers (anything but, Robert was to find out soon enough) Victoria would drive, Elizabeth was going to be away at a point to point, so Robert took this opportunity to go and see his son. He rang his ex wife to arrange things. At the end of the telephone conversation he sensed a problem. As usual she was not forthcoming but he would find out the lay of the land once he was there. Victoria and Philip insisted that he took the Range Rover. Robert was more than happy to travel by train but to save their protestations he concurred.

Chapter 5

Six o'clock Wednesday evening, Robert rang his ex to say he was in the vicinity and could call round if that was appropriate. Sandra invited him round and asked if he would like to stay for something to eat? Sandra greeted him at the door, she looked well. Robert had been to the house on a previous occasion but under more stressful conditions. She had been living with a man, Brett. A tense situation made worse by his arrival. That had been a couple years ago, since then Brett had departed, or more to the point been told to leave. Sandra had concentrated on looking after Luke her career and had generally just been a happier person. One of the things that she had accused Robert of was not being interested, so to keep the feeling of goodwill alive he now engaged her in, what he considered was idle chatter, how was her job going? "Fine" she replied and then proceeded to garnish him with all the office gossip. Robert thought to himself fuck me, I only asked how was work going. He feigned interest and thought he would risk another question, "Do you not miss having a man about the place?"

Sandra said "I'm happy enough I've got a rabbit."

Robert very happy with himself now said, "Oh, can I see it?"

Sandra smiled and said "No, I need to talk to you about something else. There is a man, in fact he is a friend of one of my friends, who, to put it bluntly is showing a little too much interest in the boys including Luke."

Robert replied, "What does your friend think?"

"She thinks he is being a gentleman, waiting before he gives her one."

"Are you sure?"

Sandra shot him a look that said do not fucking question me.

Robert remembered their arguments.

Sandra said "I'm concerned for Luke naturally but also for the other kids I'm just asking would you be able to check this man out?"

Robert, "Yes of course and Luke's fine at the moment is he?"

Sandra "Yes, all the necessary warnings have been issued, stay close to his friends and keep away from trees and bushes and so forth. The only thing is that I don't think this man operates in that way more of a slimy bastard with a cajoling manner."

Luke came in and sat next to his dad none of the excessive displays of affection, you see in the American films, hugging and kissing and I love you daddy real life was so much different. Luke was a miniature Robert. A fair-haired boy, bright blue eyes he looked like his father. He even had the same character, not a noisy child but watchful, alert.

They sat side-by-side chatting, Luke happy his dad was at home and that his parents were not arguing.

"Fancy fishing tomorrow?" Robert said

Luke responded "Yeah, we can get the bait from Arthur's."

Sandra interjected "The three of us could go for something to eat tomorrow night. There's a family pub in the next village."

Luke in bed Sandra and Robert stood on the doorstep she handed him a photograph and said, "That's him and he lives at 36 Saxon Terrace. I believe he drinks in the Crossfield Arms." Robert was impressed. The need for background information was vital.

Robert said "Leave it with me."

As a parting shot Sandra told Robert that if this man is messing about with kids then kick the shit out of him.

Robert got into his car drove a couple of streets away and consulted a local street plan. He then rang Jim. Jim was the man who had put him in touch with the Hawthorn's and was a high-ranking officer in the police force. They kept in regular touch so Jim was not surprised by his call. The pleasantries done with Robert said, "I need a favour"

Jim, delighted to be talking shop said, "Of course, what is it?"

Robert told him everything he knew, took a photo of the photo and txt'ed it to Jim, concluded the conversation by saying "I'll get back to you this evening."

Robert drove to Saxon Terrace and worked outwards from that point, located the pub, local parks and schools. He also noticed a police station not more than five minutes from the pub, by foot. It was almost half past 10 so Robert popped back to the Crossfield Arms and went in for a drink.

Fortunately it was busy, quiz night apparently and the punters were engrossed in finding out the scores. There was Terry sitting with a group of men and women, one of the crowd. The quizmaster read out the results, the team in third place were called "Boys in Blue."

Robert left the pub got into his car and parked more strategically; positioning the car behind a coupe and because of the range Rovers Height, he was afforded clear vision of the pub. The Crossfield Arms stood by itself with a car park to the rear but was surrounded by a labyrinth of alleyways. Even coming out of the front entrance a dozen steps across the road and you were back into the alleys.

11 o'clock came and went, people left the pub but not everyone left. The women who were sitting at Terry's table departed but the men didn't? He could see the Curtains being drawn in the pub effectively blacking it out. At 11:45pm a car pulled into the car park, slowly and quietly. The car was full.

Robert's phone rang, Jim.

Robert said, "What do you know?"

Jim, "The lads have been trying to crack this area for God knows how long. There is a problem that they keep coming up against a brick wall. I have explained your situation to head of operations for that district, where you're coming from but not who you are. He retires in two months and would dearly love this put to bed, so he is excepting your help."

Robert, "Should I deal with him direct?"

Jim, "Yes."

Robert, "I'll keep in touch."

While he was on the phone he had noticed some activity, approximately 250 yards directly in front of where he was sitting two men had come out of an alley crossed the road and had disappeared into another alley.

Robert turned his jacket inside out; black trousers black jeans and a black jacket, put a very dark bobble hat on and stepped out into the night.

He edged along the wall of the pub leading him to the car park; a few cars littered the tarmac. The car that had pulled in was parked very close to the back door of the pub. He was within 20 foot of the vehicle when the back door opened and out spilled a man who was clearly pissed and a young woman who was in a state of undress. The man unzipped his trousers and the woman opened a condom packet. The man seeing the condom grabbed it and flung it barking at her

"Just get on your fucking knees." heavy with Mancunian accent, he pushed her down, the woman said "You English scum I fucking hate you."

The man didn't understand this because she was a Croatian and spoke in her native language but Robert had spent some time in Croatia and had bothered to learn some of the language. He certainly understood you English scum I fucking hate you. He had heard it plenty of times before. Robert looked around him for something to throw, finding a stone he hurled it into the dark. The projectile hit a car and returned a noisy bang. The man stopped the girl and said in a loud voice said, "What's that?"

Zipping up his flies he disappeared into the car park the girl went back into the pub, probably to get another punter.

Now to catch up with the two men who were using the alleys as cover. This certainly was a quiet area; once the regulars had left the pub the streets were deserted. It was as if an evil had descended under the cover of darkness and it was only safe to come out in the daylight hours. Robert, if his bearings were correct was sure he was on the path to Terry's house. He stopped, up ahead he could hear voices, he pulled the bobble hat completely over his face, a balaclava. Crouching very low to the ground he crept forward he could clearly hear the two men. Broken English, again the Croatian accent.

Arguing, Terry was one of the men and clearly upset, but managing to keep his voice low. The Croatian was saying I promise, I promise tomorrow night I will have three young boys for you. Terry threatened him, you fucking better I've got a house full of expectant men they will not be happy. The Croatian promised again, three boys and you can do whatever you fucking want with them. With that Terry turned heel and proceeded down the alley. The Croatian stood where he was muttering under his breath in Croatian.

    Robert waited a reasonable time before making his way back along the alley. When he was back in the car he rang Alan Higgins, the contact Jim had given him. Although it was late, approaching one o'clock in the morning they arranged to meet. On the outskirts of Manchester, Robert waited and watched, Jim had given him a rough description of Alan so when he pulled in and parked he knew which car. Alan walked into the service station Robert came in after him. Robert approached Alan and introduced himself. The two men got themselves a cup of tea and sat by the window overlooking the motorway. It was godless place at this time of the morning. One or two lorry drivers making a pit stop, a couple of staff, no one who wanted to be here.

Alan spoke first at his frustration any leads and subsequent investigations had all proven to be fruitless. He did not understand. Robert told him of the night's activities. When Robert had finished Alan murmured tomorrow night it's too soon.

Robert thought to himself, Alan is fucked. He needs a hand as loathed as he was to do it he would have to bottle-feed him.

Alan, clear your head and think rationally. Do you know of a man working at the Highfield police station 6' 2", 14 stone, blonde hair with a small scar on his left cheek? Alan reiterated "small scar, that's Fletch, one of the up-and-coming stars. He is always at HQ, gets on really well with the staff."

"Any one in particular?" inquired Robert.

Alan "yeah Sean, we call them Starsky & Hutch, without them we would not have got as far as we have."

Robert sat and thought. What a farce, this man was clearly an idiot, completely out of his depth. Basic investigative questions not been asked. Probably recommended to lead the investigation by Starsky &

Hutch. Robert just wanted to chin the useless bastard. He had an idea.

Robert said, "Come out to the car, there is a phone call you need to hear."

In the car Robert connected his mobile to the speakerphone and rang Jim. The call was answered immediately "What can I do for you Robert?"

Robert did not apologise for the lateness of the call, they were cut from the same cloth.

Robert detailed the evening's events to Jim, and then finished by telling him that the man with the two nicknames was the one who raped the prostitute.

Alan piped up "You can't rape a prostitute."

Jim replied "Alan you're off the case, stay away from work, I will be there first thing tomorrow morning, Alan if I here one word of you been anywhere near the police station or being in touch with any of your colleagues you will regret it. Goodbye."

Alan objected. Jim just said "Goodbye Alan."

Jim heard the car door open and shut, and then said to Robert, "I take it he's gone."

"Yes." replied Robert

Jim, "Could you trail him."

Robert "On it."

Jim, "What about his mobile?"

Robert, "Got it."

Jim he will have two.

Robert "Got that as well, he went to the loo left his jacket behind, he is very sloppy."

Jim explained what they were to do.

Robert said, "You have only my word to go on."

Jim "No not really Robert, we have been following this for months and we were pretty close, you have just confirmed an awful lot of what we already knew, I even have the teams in place we can make the bust tomorrow evening. There are three or four houses including Terry's (that's not his real name) we need to raid. The Crossfield Arms at the centre. Unfortunately I don't need you any more, sorry.

Robert had trailed Alan back to his house while they were talking.

"Understood, just one last request. Oh by the way Alan uses cable."

When Alan had gone into his house Robert waited a couple of minutes, walked up to Alan's car and removed the tracking device.

Robert got a couple of hours sleep and was round for Luke at 7 a.m.

"Where do you want to go Luke?" Robert inquired.

Luke said, "There is an old quarry I know of, we could try there."

Robert asked, "Have you fed and watered your rabbit?" Luke puzzled "I haven't got a rabbit" Robert left it. The fishing was irrelevant; father and son having a day together nothing else really mattered. When they were on the road Luke said "Wicked car dad."

Robert smiled "It's not mine."

Luke replied "Still wicked."

During the day when he got chance he rang Sandra, explaining that he would need a favour and that he would probably have to disappear for a couple of hours that evening.

Man and boy returned at approximately 4:30 p.m., with fish but nothing worth cooking. Luke said to his mum that he needed to return a game to Jack, his mum replied go on then and straight into the bath when you get back, you smell like Grimsby.

Sandra said to Robert "I've got the makeup, let's get it done while Luke is out, and for the record you smell like Grimsby on a hot day."

When she had finished Robert to all intents and purposes looked like a Sikh. Robert said, "Well do I pass muster?"

Sandra stared at him and said, "Let's hear you talk."

"I just need to make an appearance not proclaim the coming of the prophet" Robert replied indignantly "I'll see you later."

As he left the house he could hear Sandra laughing out loud.

Robert was on his way when he got the call from Jim. They met at the designated house. Jim looked him up and down and greeted him with "How's Grimsby Mohammed?"

Robert thought to himself, piss taking bastard.

Jim said, "Let's go."

It was 5:31 p.m. by 6:04 p.m. it was all over. Five premises simultaneously raided. Robert was mightily impressed all done with military precision. Jim told Robert to come with him. In an upstairs room of the Crossfield Arms Jim was shown into a room full of men, the Croat, from last night, a couple of his hired guns, relieved of their hardware and several of Jim's men and of course Terry. All of Jim's men had their weapons trained on the suspects all except Terry. Without wasting a second Robert crossed over to Terry and gave him an almighty kick in the bollocks. He could feel the soft testicles mash. Terry collapsed to the floor and threw up. His head swimming, he thought a giant Indian smelling of fish had just attacked him, and then he passed out.

As Robert walked past Jim he said, "I'll be in touch."

Jim responded, "Sure thing Gunga."

Robert returned to the bed and breakfast he was staying at, he removed all of his clothing including the boots and placed them in a sealed plastic bag. Shaved, showered and wearing a clean set of clothes he called for Sandra and Luke. They went to the public house that Sandra had mentioned the previous evening. It was a busy establishment and while walking through the bar area Sandra could not help but notice the admiring glances that Robert took. She knew that he had seen them, he noticed everything, but it was water off a duck's back. Sandra wondered had he ever noticed her, of course he had but the real woman, maybe, maybe not.

During the evening while Luke was at the toilet,

Robert quickly relayed the earlier events, she could rest assured Terry would not be touching himself never mind anyone else for quite some time to come. Sandra said, "Julia will have to do with a rabbit."

Robert thought that Manchester must be full of furry creatures taking the place of men.

He asked Sandra if it would be possible for Luke to visit him sometime in the future. When Luke returned to the table his mum said to him "Luke would you like to visit your dad?"

Luke "Wicked."

Chapter 6

Late Friday morning and Robert was returning to the Hawthorn estate. He reread the text that Victoria had sent him. 'Friends in good form, theatre enjoyable enough Philip did not enjoy the scan. Something to do with being confined in a small space and the dull noise obviously to do with his army days.'

Then a second txt, 'elizabeth having fun, how are you? How are Luke and his mum?'

Then a third txt, 'you could answer.'

Robert thought to himself 'Yes I could have answered and believe me I wanted to because I miss you Victoria and sending texts back and forth could open the floodgates.' Robert was unsure, a new dilemma for him and these feelings for Victoria he just didn't know how to deal with them. The only thing he could say with definite certainty was he would not do anything that would jeopardise his relationship with Philip. He respected the man and hoped he in return was respected.

Robert arrived back mid-afternoon and busied himself, burnt the fishy clothes, boots and all including the plastic bag. He also cleaned the Range Rover inside and out, prepared his evening meal and got ready a sleeping bag.

While he was rolling up the sleeping bag he saw a car approaching the gates, the gates opening and the Rover speeding through and up the drive towards the house.

'Strange', he thought 'They could see the Range Rover parked outside why didn't they stop and say hello?'

He would stick his head round the door once he had parked the Range Rover up at the garages. It was Victoria making him feel slighted. Not Philip; he understood men especially military he understood why they did things and why they didn't do things but women, that was a different matter, but no that was not right, but Victoria she was confusing him.

28th April 2006 7:30 p.m.

Robert parked the Range Rover. Dusk had descended over the Hawthorn estate. The lights activated by his body heat and movement shone out from above the garages and stables across the courtyard. He could hear Desert Storm, the thoroughbred Arabian stallion, moving around, restless. A light drizzle glistened in the lights. He heard the gentle susurration that the trees whispered coming across the fields, Robert thought there is a force about tonight? Nothing is still everything is on the move. Robert entered the kitchen, no staff. He walked through the kitchen and into the hallway no one about. He carried on up to the drawing-room door, knocked and entered. Victoria was sitting by herself staring into the fire.

Robert, "Hello."

Victoria did not move, she said, "You could have answered. A simple txt, just to say hello but not you, oh no not

Robert Green."

Robert, "How is Philip?"

Victoria, "Asleep, not feeling too good."

Robert, "Where are the staff?"

Victoria, "I have given them the night off, have you done with the fucking questions?"

Robert, "No, would you like a drink?"

Victoria, relenting said, "Yes please."

Robert, "May I pour one for myself?"

Victoria, "Please do."

Robert looked at Victoria this was a very awkward situation. Even if Philip were not about they lived in different worlds.

Robert said, "If it makes things easier I will hand my notice in, I can be gone by tomorrow."

Victoria, "Why?"

Robert, "Why? Because there is a situation between us."

Victoria was enjoying this, it was the first time Robert had shown any vulnerability.

Victoria, "Situation? Please elaborate."

Robert, "I am dreadfully sorry I have totally misread the circumstances."

Victoria, "Situation, what fucking situation."

Robert beginning to squirm, "Oh God."

Victoria, "Let me, you think I have fallen for you, Philip is your boss and I am a woman who has a position to maintain, am I right."

Robert, "Oh God."

Victoria, "Seems to me, for all your machismo, when it comes to love you have not got a clue."

Robert, "Oh God."

Victoria "Let's keep god out of it for the moment, do you love me."

Robert stared with a blank expression.

Victoria, "I will take that as a yes which is just as well because I am rather fond of you. Robert please answer my txts, I was worried about you. You know as well as I do nothing will happen between us while there is breath to be drawn in Philip's body but that does not mean I can not think of you, I can not worry about you and can not long for you. This is difficult, life's like that. I would rather see you every day and go through the full gamut of emotions than to not have you in my world. Was that roughly the gist of what you were trying to say Robert?"

Robert reeling, "Yes."

Victoria, "Good, we sing from the same hymn sheet."

Robert struggling to find anything sensible to say asked Victoria what a rabbit was.

Victoria looking bemused said, "A small furry mammal." Robert continued "I know that, when I asked Sandra if she missed having a man around the house she told me she had a rabbit."

Victoria "Oh, I see." and started to laugh.

Later that evening Robert stood alone in the wooded area close to his house. His eyes grew accustomed to the darkness and he began to prepare his night's sleeping quarters. He enjoyed being outside it wasn't the first time he had done this since arriving at the Hawthorns and it wouldn't be the last.

Robert wandered through the woods, barely visible he could hear the running water from the small river on the other side of the trees, his body moved in time with nature. His intimate knowledge of his surroundings was a powerful force. Wherever he had been while in the army he felt at ease with mother earth. She had looked after him, providing food and shelter. Now mother earth had a rival, Victoria. For all the unharnessed power earth possessed it did not, could not move his heart. He would do everything he could to ensure he remained in Victoria's thoughts.

Later Robert sent Victoria a txt. She replied within seconds. 'Philip is asleep in next room. i will xplain soon. im reading but restless. how are you darling? of course this message will be deleted, immediately. X'

Robert's reply. 'im also restless but happy. you have changed my world. i know what a rabbit is. i fear i have a lot of catching up to do. never been called darling before. I like it. what should I call you?'

Victoria's reply, 'call me anything you like, don't ask me. goodnight darling. c u 2moro x'

Robert. 'goodnight X'

Robert woke with the first light. He walked down to the river and washed his face in the clear running water. On the other side of the river a Roe deer was chewing on young shoots, shedding its winter coat. Much like Robert he needed to shed his old ways. He went back to his overnight pitch tidied his belongings away and left the scene as If nobody had ever visited there. He went back to his house changed into a pair of shorts and trainers and went running. He felt alive, the cool morning air hitting his skin the rhythmic beat of his trainers against the earth. He ran for an hour, he had never run so fast for so far.

Later that morning Robert entered the kitchen of the house. He gave a cheery good morning to all the staff present. Brenda smiled and said, "Got lucky with one of the villagers."

Robert moving through the kitchen replied, "No." and stepped out into the hallway.

Victoria was standing at the foot of the stairs ready to go up and see Philip. Robert asked her how he was faring. Victoria replied, "He is much better thank you, I guess he was tired after a couple of busy days. He should be down soon."

Elizabeth arrived back on Sunday afternoon, Robert wasted no time in asking if he could take Desert Storm out the following morning. Elizabeth said, "Of course you can, he desperately needs a workout and I find it difficult to handle him."

Robert thought for a second before saying, "How was your weekend, how did you get on?"

Elizabeth, "The weekend was splendid thank you and I did not fall off so all in all a success."

6 a.m. the next morning.

Robert mounted Desert Storm, sensing he was about

to be cut loose the horse reared up. Carlton, the stable lad, ducked for cover shouting out, "You're fucking mad, the pair of you."

The horse bolted for the open gate. Although it looked as though the horse was running wild Robert was in control of him. He was probably the only man on the estate with the strength to steer Desert Storm. They headed for the small gallop on the other side of the field. Once on the run Robert gave the animal its head. This was better than any machine. The pure exhilaration, the power generated was incredible Robert could feel the horse's heartbeat, blood pumping muscle stretched to breaking point. After just one lap of the gallop he slowed the horse, this animal would run until he dropped, now he could feel his own heart thumping, he hadn't realised the sheer thrill of the ride. At the entrance he could see Victoria, Elizabeth and Carlton. Robert jumped off Desert Storm and walked the last couple of hundred yards to the entrance.

As he approached Elizabeth teasingly said, "Seems to me Storm was not the only one who needed a workout."

Carlton quickly unsaddled the horse and put a blanket over the horses sweating back. Elizabeth and Carlton led the horse back to its stable. Victoria said to Robert, "Feel better for that darling?"

Robert replied, "Yes, I do."

Victoria warned Robert, "Philip is looking out of the window he is not spying just interested in what is going on, he will be back in bed fairly soon."

Robert asked Victoria how she was.

She stopped, looked at Robert and said, "Concerned, we will get the results in a couple of days. He is always very tired now, hard to know what to do."

They carried on walking toward the house when Victoria added, "I know this must be frustrating for you but just do not kill the horse."

Dr Kneebone came to see the Hawthorns on Wednesday afternoon. He did not leave till early evening and when Robert went up to the house it was a sombre scene that he encountered. Philip explained to him, "I have been diagnosed with multiple sclerosis. Rare in someone as old as me but apparently the eye episode many years ago was an initial attack and it has lain dormant ever since."

Philip went silent so Victoria carried on, "There is no cure, the MS will take its own course. By that I mean you cannot predict what and when things will happen. What will happen is anybody's guess, apparently no two people are the same. Kneebone says carry on living your life as normal, when you are tired rest, and avoid stress. In fact stress could have caused the forgetfulness. Nobody wants to be ill," Victoria glanced at Philip, "but it is here and we will deal with it." Now looking at Robert, "All of us family and friends."

A chronic illness which no one can predict its path. The consultant explained it's many and varied symptoms. The only advice he could really give them was to use a physiotherapist and live life as normally as possible, that old cliché 'take each day as it comes' was never truer.

Chapter 7

April was a grey month, but May was something else. Beautiful warm, sunny days. Elizabeth was invited to many balls and had many admirers. She had much to do to transcend her mother's beauty but as the years passed by she would ably be her mother's daughter.

Towards the end of May Victoria spoke with Robert, "Elizabeth is going to a ball next Friday, I would like you to drive her there and home again."

Robert a little surprised said, "Yes of course, any particular reason?"

Victoria, "She is not attending this ball with her regular friends, the invite has come through a convoluted series of phone calls. The people inviting her are Thomas's friends, Thomas will not be there so why she has been invited is beyond me. Elizabeth is saying it will be fine so stop worrying."

The problem being that Victoria did not know these people, in fact she had not seen Thomas for the best part of a year. Such was Elizabeth's innocent nature she had expected the invite even though she had only met this chap once or twice before and only very briefly.

Elizabeth rebuffed her mother's concern with a glib "Do not be silly."

May 26, 2006

Robert drove Elizabeth to the Grange hotel in London. He was to wait until Elizabeth's companions had arrived and then go to the Sheraton and wait for Elizabeth's call to collect her.

At 10:30 p.m. Robert could see Elizabeth and her acquaintances make their way towards the Sheraton. Robert could see the age difference quite clearly self-assured young women and overconfident young men made Elizabeth look like a schoolgirl.

At 11:30 p.m. a prearranged call was made to Elizabeth's mobile. This activated the transmitter placed inside the cell phone by Robert, which in turn was inside a very small handbag hanging from Elizabeth's wrist.

Inside the car Robert could quite clearly hear any person talking with in the vicinity of the phone. The female members of the party left Elizabeth alone this was probably due to jealousy or she just was not on their wavelength, unfortunately the door was open for the young men to try their luck. Elizabeth persistently refused any offer of a drink soft or alcoholic. Until Richard (the original invite) and Isaac kept pestering for her to have a drink. At 1:45 a.m. Elizabeth relented, saying, "Ok, one small glass of wine, and then I am going."

As soon as Robert heard this exchange he was on his feet. He smelt a rat, why be so insistent on giving a girl a drink so late at night? As well as the listening device Robert had also placed a tracker on the inside of Elizabeth's bag. Robert stepped into the lobby of the Sheraton, it was mayhem and to make matters worse the majority of people were dressed in black and white. The scene resembled feeding time at the Penguin zoo.

He was still listening to his mobile. Elizabeth and

the two men were now in a quieter place, she was trying to talk but struggling. Robert walked forwards stepping round and over various bodies in various positions some by themselves and some entwined taking a stab at romance! Robert kept moving forward up steps past function rooms, turning right he came across the first bedrooms. They were close and they had got Elizabeth on the bed.

He heard Richard say, "Do not bother undressing her I will pull her dress up." Followed by Isaac " Lucky you, stockings and a thong."

Richard "You just get the fucking mobile ready then we can send the evidence straight to that arsehole Thomas, he will have to pay. So you would not accept a drink you stuck up little bitch."

At that moment Robert reached the room, wasting no time he kicked the door open. He stepped inside to a scene he really did not want to see. Elizabeth virtually unconscious lying facedown on the bed dress pulled up above her waist. A busboy's trolley that had been used to transport Elizabeth back to the room. He walked over to the photographer took his mobile grabbed him and physically moved Isaac to Richard. Robert then asked both of them to empty their pockets, which they willingly did. No way did they want to upset this madman any further. Richard held out a small empty packet. Robert asked, "What was in this?"

All of a sudden Richard was no longer the mighty mouth. Robert with visible signs of his patience wearing thin asked again, Isaac said, "Rohypnol."

Robert looked at Elizabeth. He shouldn't have done, the anger that he felt towards these tossers welled up inside him and exploded on to their chins. They didn't know what had hit them. With a satisfying cracking of bones first Richard slumped to the floor followed by Isaac. Robert knew that this pair of wankers would be sucking through straws for some time to come.

Robert pulled down Elizabeth's dress and picked her up. In the hallway he headed for the back of the hotel. There were plenty of staff around but frankly they were not bothered by another socialite who had drunk too much and now needed to go home to mummy to look after her.

As Robert approached the kitchens he bumped into a Middle Eastern woman coming out. He asked her if she would look after Elizabeth for a few minutes. The woman spoke very little English but seemed to understand. When Robert sat Elizabeth on the floor and against the wall the woman knelt down beside her and held her hand.

Robert sprinted back down the hallway and through the lobby, where he noticed a young man throwing up into a pot plant, a member of the hotel staff trying to talk to him. Once outside a quick sprint 100 yards down the road and he was in the car. Bearing in mind how late it was or how early, depending on how you view 24 hours in a day, it was still busy, Robert reversed the wrong way down a one-way road and hand braked turned into the delivery area of the Sheraton. Pulling alongside the kitchen doors Robert jumped out of the car ran through the kitchen and through the doors, which led to where he had left Elizabeth. The woman was still comforting her. Robert took a £50 note out of his pocket and gave it to her. She said something in her native tongue, which Robert guessed was Iranian, picked up Elizabeth and was safely back in the car and heading for home by 2:12 a.m. A few miles outside of London Robert pulled into a lay-by and removed the tracker from Elizabeth's bag and the transmitter from her mobile.

On his way again he called Victoria. He told her

to call the family doctor and to have him at the house by 3:30 a.m. and to tell him that Elizabeth may have ingested the drug Rohypnol.

He then rang Jim and asked if it were possible to have a police escort. Within 10 minutes a patrol car came alongside Robert, the driver signalled for Robert to go ahead. Robert pushed the car along to 130 miles per hour. The patrol car easily kept pace with him.

Jim rang back, "Every thing ok Robert?"

Robert, "I hope so."

He went on to explain what had happened with Elizabeth. Jim asked where the two men were. Robert could only guess that maybe they were still at the hotel possibly still in the room. Jim said, "I will need to speak to Philip, what time do you think you will be back at the house?"

Robert replied, "If I keep at this speed 40 minutes."

The ever-forward thinking Jim responded, "Ok, I will call you in one hour."

Victoria called "Robert, the doctor will be here just after three. How is Elizabeth?"

Robert "Sleeping, I know it is late but I have been speaking to Jim Coldershot and he would like to speak to Philip in say 30 minutes, would that be okay?"

Victoria responded in the affirmative.

The patrol car left Robert at the gates of the house. Approaching the house he reflected on the good and the bad aspects of life. For all the chaos and mayhem that existed in every city in every country there were the good people. The people who worked nine to five, who washed their cars and mowed their lawns at the weekend. Take these people out of the equation and all that would be left is anarchy. These steady Eddie's must once have been the chaos and only by living through that mindless phase matured into law-abiding adults. But this was a rapidly changing world and there seemed to be a definite split growing between good and evil, them and us. It was becoming increasingly difficult to tell who was who, who was right and who was wrong. Would this restless earth ever grow up?

He knew one thing for sure those two bastards he left

in the hotel room got off very lightly.

Robert pulled up along side the steps. The front door of the house opened and out came Philip and Victoria, followed by the doctor and a nurse. Robert carried Elizabeth in his arms. He didn't stop he moved forward with purpose. Victoria fell into step with him on his right-hand side and Philip on his left. Victoria had her hand on her daughter's forehead, Robert knew she was crying. Through the doors, up the stairs, along the hall way and into Elizabeth's bedroom the small group of people moved as one. Intense concern for the one person who was completely oblivious to this scene.

Robert placed Elizabeth on her bed and left the room.

A few moments later Philip appeared with the doctor who had a question for Robert.

"Was she sexually assaulted?"

Robert knew that the dreaded question was coming, "No." he replied.

Robert's mobile rang it was Jim. Robert said to Philip

"Were you aware that Jim wanted to speak to you?" Philip nodded and took the phone from Robert. Philip walked further down the hallway and sat in one of the comfortable chairs that you would think was put there for such occasions. The doctor had disappeared back into the bedroom leaving Robert alone. He went downstairs and sat in the drawing-room for what seemed like an eternity. In this time he decided he must tell Philip and Victoria the truth. If nothing had happened then nothing need be said about the bugs but something had happened and Philip was no fool.

He heard voices outside. The doctor and the nurse were leaving.

Philip and Victoria came into the sitting room. Robert asked, "How is Elizabeth?"

A relieved Victoria said,

"She is fine, heavily sedated by the Rohypnol and will probably have a dreadful hangover tomorrow but fine."

Robert apologised for letting their daughter be subjected to such a horrific ordeal and he fully understood if they wanted to let him go, Philip interjected, in a calming voice he said, "Robert, Robert and if we had stuck by the original plan which was for Elizabeth to be dropped off, meet with these people and spend the night in London. What would have become of her? No, I will not hear of you leaving us."

Philip sat in deep thought for a short while, Robert could hear the house moaning and creaking as if preparing itself for a statement. Philip mused, "Victoria and I are a little confused on two points, why did you chin the bastards and how did you know?"

Robert explained, "When I saw Elizabeth laying on the bed, such an innocent, vulnerable and trusting girl I exploded which I know is very unprofessional but I did and that's that. How did I know, I bugged her phone and put a tracker in her bag. Why did I do that? Both of you were overly concerned. You did not really know these people, they are older than Elizabeth and she was going to be out of my sight for long periods during the evening. Yet again if this is unacceptable I will tender my resignation but whatever happens you need to hear this."

Robert had recorded the conversation between Richard and Isaac. As the little machine played out the recording he could see any colour remaining in Philip's and Victoria's faces completely drain away. When the machine stopped Philip slumped back into his seat. Victoria got up and sat on the arm of Philip's chair, held his hand in her hands and for the second time cried.

Robert asked, "What should I do?"

Victoria looked up, forced a smile and said, "Coffee would be good."

In the kitchen Robert stared out of the window onto the stables. It was 5 a.m., dawn was doing it's damndest to spread light onto this darkest of nights. Victoria came into the kitchen "Philip has gone to bed, he cannot believe that Thomas has stooped so low as to do such a terrible thing to his sister."

The coffee pot boiled, the aroma pervading their senses. Robert opened the back door allowing the outside to come in and hopefully alleviate some of the pain. Robert and Victoria sat at the kitchen table. Finally Victoria, in a thin voice uttered, "What do you think happened?"

Robert, not knowing an easy way to say what was on

his mind could only speak truthfully what he believed to be the truth, and plainly, so as not to be misunderstood said, "I don't know if Elizabeth is a virgin or not. I do not need to know or want to know but it sounds like a bet has taken place with proof supplied that she lost her virginity while someone watched and took photos."

Victoria, crying again, nodded her head. She looked longingly at Robert and then said, "I wish you could hold me darling, I know that is incredibly self-indulgent of me especially at a time like this, so I will stand strong and firm, have a shower, a cup of tea, read the Sundays' and be there for when my family wake up, stop crying be the wife, the mother."

Victoria stood, as did Robert, he moved around to Victoria's side of the table, collected her empty coffee cup and in one movement moved his head close to her ear. She was trembling, at that moment he could smell the woman, her body heat, her natural warmth and with every molecule of his being working overtime he resisted the urge to hold her, he whispered "I love you."

As Robert moved towards the sink and Victoria towards the door that led out to the hallway he turned towards Victoria saying, "What do we tell the staff?"

Without hesitation she said, "Elizabeth ate something that disagreed with her, consequently we have been up all night and you, well you just do not sleep do you."

Victoria disappeared through the door Robert left alone in the kitchen noticed how hard his heart was beating, not even when he was toe to toe with the enemy did this happen.

Just then Alan and Deirdre came through the open door.

Robert called out, "Morning folks, Elizabeth has been ill during the night. Philip and Victoria have not had much sleep and I am just about to take the dogs out, will explain more when I return."

Later that evening Robert made his way into the house, the last of the kitchen staff had left and all that remained was the smell of cooking. This resonated with Robert; the house had its own identity life breathed into it by the Hawthorn family and although Philip was the recognised master it was Victoria who held it all together.

Robert walked through the kitchen up the hallway and in his usual manner knocked on the drawing-room door. When he entered Elizabeth almost knocked him off his feet putting her arms around him she kissed him on the cheek. Understandably she thanked him again and again. Then she added, "You know what colour knickers I wear."

Philip groaned, "Dear God."

Robert looked at Victoria for help, she aided him, "We followed your lead. Honesty now, rather than hear it through the grapevine because believe it or not the gossip is just as ripe amongst this class of people as anywhere else if not worse."

Philip suggested they retire to the library for a peaceful drink. Robert concurred.

In the library Robert asked Philip how he was.

Philip answered, "Not too good."

Robert pondered, "In what respect."

Philip took a sip of his whisky before answering, "Fatigued, the warm weather does not seem to agree with me and if I am not mistaken I have now got a noticeable tremor in my left hand."

Philip going off on a tangent spoke about the conflict in the Middle East and they chatted like this on and off for the next hour and a half. Robert noticed however that Philip was uncomfortable. He assumed you would be just after finding out what your son had planned for your daughter.

Then Philip dumbfounded Robert by saying, "If anything happens to me will you promise that the girls will be looked after?"

Robert sat in amazed silence, struggling with the enormity of the request he thought best to clarify.

"And by the girls you mean Victoria and Elizabeth?"

Philip, raising his voice, "Good God man, I do not mean the fucking sheep."

Robert didn't really have a life plan and apart from Victoria he hadn't thought much about the future. There may never be a future with Victoria but for the moment he was happy just to be close to her. With this in mind he said to Philip "Of course I will but you have no intentions of falling off this mortal coil."

After a while Philip responded,

"No, I have not but god knows what my son has planned for me."

With that Philip finished off his drink and retired for the evening.

Chapter 8

Towards the end of June the Hawthorns announced they were to be on holiday through July and August. A friend had offered them the use of his boat in the South of France; no plans had been made because of Philips health but they had taken the consultant's advice on board. To live each day as it comes.

Philip, Victoria, Elizabeth and a friend, Alan and Josie were to make up the party. Philip said to Robert, "We would very much like you to come as well?"

Robert thought for a second before answering, "I would really like that but Luke will be spending some time with me during the summer holidays."

Philip without a second thought said, "Bring him."

Robert replied, "Ok, but I will have to clear it with his mother first."

The party flew out on the 12th of July 2006, Philip insisting that they all go together. Victoria confided in Robert that Philip was struggling, the warm May and a hot start to July had really slowed him down. Philip, ever the optimist dug deep and kept going, having to rest frequently. The size of the party travelling together was really an insurance policy by Philip. Safety in numbers.

They set up camp in the Villa of the friend who owned the boat. Such were the vagaries of multiple sclerosis Philip picked up. To all intents and purposes he shouldn't have. It was a damn sight hotter in the South of France than back home.

Sitting on the edge of the pool Robert surveyed the scene, Elizabeth and her friend Scarlet, sunning themselves and even though everyone was told to enjoy themselves, Alan stayed close to Philip and spoke with him, Josie did not need a second invite and splashed in the water with Luke.

Victoria sat next to Robert and said, "Enjoying the view?"

Robert looked over his shoulder at the backdrop of the mountains responded, "They are rather beautiful."

Victoria teasingly replied, "She is, is she not?"

A perplexed Robert said, "Do you know these mountains by name?"

Victoria feigning confusion, "I am sorry but I think we are at crossed purposes. I was talking about Scarlett, what were you talking about?"

Robert, "You know full well I was talking about the mountains and yes Scarlett is a beautiful woman but young."

Victoria disappeared into the water leaving Robert to question his naiveté regarding women. He looked at Elizabeth and Scarlet both beautiful young women, and although they were the same age Elizabeth came across as an innocent young girl.

One more day of rest at the Villa and then they would head out to the boat.

9:00a.m Saturday 15th of July 2006, the party

collected by speedboat made their way out to sea. After several minutes Luke said to his dad, "Is that it?"

Robert looking through binoculars read the name Annabella II he said to Luke, "I believe it is."

The boat, a 120ft launch looked exquisite. When everyone had boarded Robert said to Victoria

"What happened to Annabella I?"

Victoria replied, "The Hammersteins are on it."

Robert tried a joke, "Buy one get one free" and wished he hadn't.

"No" said Victoria "for all mine and Philip's wealth and that is considerable we are nothing compared to the Hammersteins. The Annabella I is to say the least impressive."

Robert sheepishly apologised for his blunder and told her he did not mean to offend their friends.

Victoria replied rather sharply, "You have nothing to apologise for, you were not to know. If men were as honest and noble as you, there would not be the problems there are in the world today."

Victoria realising that her feelings for Robert were spilling forth added, "Crummy joke."

Victoria smiled, turned heel and went to find the others.

After an hour everyone gathered on the main deck. The captain introduced himself, William Bennett but he preferred to be known as Bill. William and Philip knew each other from way back, so informality was the order of the day. Bill then went on to introduce the crew, six including him, the facilities aboard the boat of which there were many; hot tub, dinghy, two jet skis and a small speedboat. Finally he went on to explain that the boat and the crew were completely at their disposal. They chose the destinations or they could stay where they were it was entirely up to them.

Philip took his cue, "Luke what would you like to do today?" He looked to his dad and said in a low voice "Dingy, jet skis."

Philip almost shouted with a sense of relief, "Excellent

choice. Bill we will stay here today, the youngsters can play and I can rest."

For the rest of that day Philip sat in the shade and let the sea breeze cool his body the others played as instructed. In the hot tub, on the dinghy, on the jet skis and swam in the sea. Robert took great delight in showing his son how to use the dinghy and the jet skis.

At the end of the day everyone ate together. Robert noticed that there was absolutely no class distinction and how Scarlet fell into this utopia. He wondered did the Hawthorns choose their friends very carefully or did like-minded people attract each other. A mixture of the two, probably.

By anyone's standards the next two days were idyllic. Bill took them to secluded coves, they visited small fishing villages, swam in the clear warm water and ate at the local restaurants. Even Alan donned a pair of shorts and waded into the surf much to Josie's amusement who tried to pull him under the water. Cautious Alan backed out of the water and stood on the beach daring Josie to try but she remembered her place and backed down.

Philip and Luke spent some time fishing, caught a

couple of tiddlers and spent more time measuring them to see who had caught biggest fish. In the afternoons when the temperature began to rise the girls disappeared to the upper deck to sit in the sun. Philip dozed, Luke under Robert's guidance snorkelled, Alan and Josie spent some time with the boat's crew, Alan trying to ensure everything was correct for Philip and Victoria. He need not have worried but the crew took on his concerns.

One afternoon while Luke was busy doing nothing Robert sought out Victoria. She sat alone in the dining area reading a book.

As Robert entered he said to Victoria, "Any good?"

Victoria put down the book and gestured for Robert to sit next to her. Once Robert was comfortable she said, "It is about MS and one woman's plan to beat it."

Robert thought for a second, "Define beating it?"

Victoria considered her answer, "Well I have not finished the book yet but from what I have read I think it is more about managing the disease."

Robert genuinely interested said, "And how is Philip

managing?"

Victoria, "Very good, he does all the right things, rests when he is tired, and avoids stress, which of course means not to get worked up about world affairs. His diet is good, he does not smoke and although he likes a drop of Scotch he really does not drink that much. I know my physiotherapy skills are limited but I try my best to keep his muscles exercised to stimulate blood flow. It is only for a few weeks and then he will be back to the real thing. Luke is good for him, treats your son like a grandson. This holiday is just what the doctor ordered. As long as he stays out of the direct sunlight at the hottest time of the day he is coping very well."

"Is he sleeping at the moment?" Robert inquired. Victoria looking straight into Robert's eyes said, "Yes, why? Are you going to talk dirty to me?"

Robert looking at his feet mumbled, "No."

Victoria laughed, "Oh Robert I can turn you into a schoolboy at the drop of a hat. You do know I am teasing."

Victoria picking up from an earlier conversation

continued, "By the way you might not be looking at Scarlett but she is definitely looking at you."

"I am aware of that" Robert said "but to be perfectly honest I do not translate that into a sexual meaning. I know this is a holiday but my priorities have not changed. The well-being of this group of people at this moment in time is uppermost in my mind."

Victoria touched by Robert's sincerity replied, "You really are something else Robert and I fully appreciate all that you do and will do for us but let me explain something to you. You are single, 6'1" 6'2" 13-ish stone and have the body of an athlete. All you have worn during the day on this boat is shorts, and if I say so myself you are a good-looking chap so do not be surprised if a 20-year-old girl, although I would define Scarlett as a young woman, is looking at you with thoughts of an intimate nature. I know there are only good intentions coming from you but it all adds to the attraction and by the way the scars on your shoulder lead one to think you could be dangerous. Even more of an attraction."

Leaning closer to Robert Victoria whispered, "I should know."

The 18th of July 2006.

The day started out much the same as the previous two. Everyone was happy to stay where they were, giving Philip a rest day. Bill was explaining to Robert the mechanics and the running of the boat, happy to have found someone who was interested and understood the intricacies. Both men looked up at the same time and Bill called to Philip, "Expecting company?"

Philip walked over to the two men and watched as a small boat approached. Philip groaned, "Oh god."

Robert called Victoria. She came to the small group of men. The little boat was now alongside the Annabella, Victoria said to no one in particular, "Thomas."

Victoria took Philip back into the shade to sit down.

Three people boarded the Annabella. A more suspicious group of people you would hope not to see. A tall African looking man who looked as if he could handle himself. He did not speak to anyone and his unsmiling countenance deterred any interaction. A woman who must be a prostitute; her clothes, pallor and demeanour spoke of neglect, abuse and of little hope. It was the third person, Thomas, who drew the eye. Where his sister was a beautiful vibrant and innocent person Thomas was none of these things.

Robert was surprised at how small Thomas was no more than 5' 6", black curly hair, in stark contrast to his pale, maybe white skin, and thin, too thin. Like a cheap plastic doll to be found in the pound shop Thomas gave the impression that he had been left behind and another doll had been favoured. That was the image Thomas was trying to portray and he almost carried it off. Save for his clothes an old T-shirt, mismatched with an even older pair of shorts and a pair of sandals that looked like they had been rescued from a skip. As Robert scrutinised him he realised that fair enough the clothes were old but were far from inexpensive. Designer apparel could not be passed off as rags because of its age. A fashion critique was not required to see how expensive his sunglasses were. Strange, Robert thought, to go to such lengths to give the image of impoverishment only then to blow the whole thing with a £300 or £400 pair of shades. Maybe Thomas was saying 'look at me down in the mouth but if you look close enough I have money.'

Thomas walked over to Philip and Victoria and in a sneering manner said, "Hear you're not too well father, what are the quacks saying?"

Philip was about to answer him but Thomas continued, he was not interested in his question to Philip and certainly not interested in any thing he had to say. Thomas enquired, "Is there any food on board? Can you arrange for a servant to bring out salmon?"

Victoria said, "Of course, who are your friends Thomas?"

A dismissive Thomas said, "I have no friends."

Victoria in a vain attempt to engage with her son said, "I will arrange for the berths to be re-organised so that there is room for you and your two colleagues." Thomas snapped back at his mother, "Colleagues? Do not flatter yourself mother, we will not be staying."

Thomas, the African and the prostitute sat with their legs dangling in the hot tub. A crewmember brought out a selection of food and drink, the prostitute devoured most of it. Even among such a small group the African and the prostitute distanced themselves from Thomas.

Robert had through his years in service and especially

the SAS learned to make judgments as quickly as possible. So it was with Thomas, here was an individual who lived in a contradiction. On first viewing he gave the impression that he was down on his luck but when you scratched the surface he was far from that. Designer clothes, posh accent, posher than the rest of his family. A substantial allowance from Philip and Victoria, porche gathering dust in the garage at home, first-class education and the most wonderful parents. A loving and caring sister raised together how could they be so different. Robert's sociology was based on action; even in planned operations circumstances changed in a second. To sit and think what made a person what they were was alien to him. Thomas was bad and he would do whatever he thought needed to be done to get what he wanted. He had no friends, he resented his family and someone was going to pay for the way he was.

Robert looked around the Annabella. It was deadly quiet, in fact the only people visible were Thomas and his two acquaintances. Robert went inside and found Victoria. He asked her how Philip was. Without looking directly at Robert Victoria answered "He is lying down in his cabin."

"Victoria" Robert said to get her attention. "For

what it is worth I will give you some advice. Get everyone together including Philip and go back outside and continue as normal. I will guarantee you that Thomas and his two buddies will not like it and move. Somewhere along the line drugs are involved, maybe the African looking chap, definitely the girl who looks like a prostitute and more than likely Thomas but we can't see his eyes and the eyes tell all."

Victoria started to apologise for Thomas and that Elizabeth had let on to him where they were and everything was such a mess. Robert interrupted her in mid flow, "Please Victoria, let us help Philip and try to get this holiday back on track but before we do anything a warning. If they are taking drugs they will be unpredictable so beware."

Victoria did all she was asked to do and within an hour the parties had changed places. Thomas, the African and the prostitute had disappeared into one of the cabins and everyone else was outside enjoying themselves but keeping a watchful eye on the door to see when they would emerge again. The rest of the day passed peacefully and afternoon turned into evening. The party decided to stay on board and to eat on deck. The table was set with an extra three spaces available but they did not appear.

Luke persuaded his dad to go night fishing on the dinghy. Robert agreed even though he knew there was no night fishing to be had in these waters.

The dinghy bobbed about in close proximity to the Annabella. Robert and Luke chatted, Robert asked Luke what sort of fish he was looking for. Luke replied, "Big fish." Robert smiled and said "Big fish, well we can but hope." Robert stopped talking and listened intently. A vessel was approaching the port side of the Annabella. Luke heard it as well and like his father stayed quiet. Using the paddle Robert edged closer to the Annabella. Voices could be heard quite clearly and the main voice was Thomas. The vessel, a small yacht, was now alongside the Annabella, Thomas called out, "Baptiste."

Response, in a heavy French accent "Aah, Thomas how are you my friend?"

Thomas dispensing with the pleasantries said, "I trust you have the goods? Baptiste shrugging off Thomas's bad manners, "Yes of course but will you not introduce me to such lovely company?" Baptiste was of course referring to Victoria, Elizabeth and Scarlett, Thomas again ignoring Baptiste's attempt at conversation shouted, "When I see the goods."

Baptiste maintaining a jovial manner replied, "Let us not be hasty Thomas, your reputation is to say a little flawed and you will not be seeing any goods until I see the money. If there are problems I have three men with me who will sort out any discrepancies. Please note Thomas they carry crossbows not guns, we do not want to wake the neighbour's do we."

On hearing this Robert whispered to Luke, "You have your mobile and you know how to operate this dinghy, I want you to head for the harbour and once there to wait for my call but first we will move closer to the boat's bow."

Once at the bow Robert strapped a knife to his calf and got into the water.

On the boat Thomas asked his father for money. Philip said, "Thomas I do not have any money with me."

Thomas barely contained himself, "Fucking great, as soon as I need something, as soon as I ask for help you let me down. If she (pointing at Elizabeth) wants she gets." Thomas thought for a moment, "You always carried a lot of money with you, how come you have none now?"

Philip in exasperation, "That was a long time ago and for completely different reasons to dealing in drugs."

Thomas relishing the thought of making his father squirm, "Yes father, the man who is going to carry on the family name is a drugs dealer."

Just then Luke gunned the dinghy engine, like a magnet it drew everyone from starboard to the port side. Disappearing very quickly towards land the dinghy masked by blackness could just be made out. Thomas screamed, "Who was that?"

Victoria heart pounding could hardly believe her eyes she managed to whisper, "Robert."

Thomas beginning to lose control, "Who the fuck is Robert?"

Victoria, holding onto the side of the Annabella for dear life as if the boat could save her, trying desperately to maintain her composure uttered, "Robert is a man who helps at the house." As Victoria spoke these words her belief in Robert drained away.

By now Robert was under the bow of the yacht.

Swimming underwater he reached the far side of the boat and began to swim towards the stern.

Baptiste called out to Thomas, "Thomas my patience is wearing thin. Tell me what that noise was and I possibly have a solution to your money problems."

Now stood on the starboard side everyone listened in eager anticipation to what Thomas was about to say.

Thomas, "The noise was the sound of the dinghy and a coward making a run for it."

Philip angrily interrupted, "Robert is not a coward."

"Well where is he?" Thomas sneered at his father, "Robert as you affectionately call the gorilla and that bastard kid have left you to fend for yourself."

Philip enraged at what Thomas was saying and partly because it seemed to be true took a swing at Thomas. Philip missed and stumbled onto the deck. The sound of laughter could be heard coming from the small yacht.

Just then Alan collapsed to the deck in agony clasping his arm, blood pouring from the wound made by the crossbow bolt. The 12-inch projectile bolt protruded from both sides of his arm.

Robert surfaced, a few feet ahead of where the steps leading up to the boats deck. He could hear Alan groaning and the voices of Victoria and Josie offering words of comfort.

Then he heard Baptiste say, "Thomas you toe rag, perhaps I can have your full attention now. I knew you would be a problem so I have arranged for another dealer to take the goods but not to completely have wasted a trip I will take those two women off your hands."

Baptiste pointed at Scarlet and Victoria, Thomas retorted, "You can have them but I need the goods."

In a weak voice Philip said, "Have you no shame."

Thomas eyes wide open screeched at Phillip, "Shame**!** Is that my shame or your shame at turning your son into this."

The African grabbed Scarlet and Victoria by the arms and forced them to the steps. Baptiste could be heard saying, "Thank God for a little common sense."

Thomas approached the African pleading with him to get the drugs before releasing the women to Baptiste. The African let go of Victoria so that he could belt Thomas across his face with the back of his hand. Thomas fell to the deck still imploring the African to do as he asked.

As Robert reached the deck of the yacht everyone's eyes were on the African and Thomas. The suited Baptiste and his three men stood in a line, moving quickly across the deck Robert knew he had to act decisively. While on the move he took the knife from the strapping and on reaching the first man he ran the knife across the back of the knee cutting the tendons. As the man fell to the deck Robert removed the crossbow from his grip. Already loaded he shot the next man in the thigh. As he fell Robert again relieved him of his loaded crossbow. The third man was turning to face the unwelcome attacker but all the years of training came into the reckoning. While the man was turning Robert was moving and he shot the third man through the foot pinning him to the deck. Robert grabbed the crossbow and shot the bolt into the deck as he turned Baptiste was reaching inside his jacket. Like an exert from a kung fu film Robert moved quickly across the deck towards Baptiste and he felt Robert's foot connect with the side of his head and a fist crack his nose. Baptiste crashed to the deck. Robert did a quick body check of the assailants, tied them together and threw the crossbows over to the Annabella.

With the four men secured Robert looked over at the Annabella. The small yacht was almost touching the bigger boat. He could see that the African now had hold of Scarlett. Robert leapt from the small yacht to the Annabella a considerable jump upwards, grabbed hold of the railings and swung himself onto the Annabella deck. The African produced a knife and held it against Scarlett's neck.

Robert spoke with Philip about what to do with the other boat and its crew. Although there was not much of a response from Philip, Robert kept speaking. This threw the African, who fully expecting Robert to try and help Scarlett lowered the knife. Robert never lost sight of the terrified girl. He moved over to the table they had been dining at and started to drink from a small beer bottle. Still maintaining a conversation with Philip he said, "I'm paid to look after the Hawthorns' anyone else is outside of my remit."

The African lowered the knife even further, realising he had the wrong woman, at which point Robert took hold of the bottle by the neck, and in one movement it was sent spinning towards the African's head.

The black man watched the bottle all the way until it crashed against his skull. Releasing the knife, letting go of Scarlett and collapsing to the deck happened in one flowing movement. Scarlett ran to Robert and hugged him. Robert prising himself free of the grateful female called out to Philip, "We have some things to sort out; Alan, that boat, its casualties, Thomas and his acquaintances and I need to get Luke back, which I will do immediately."

Robert called Luke on his mobile.

Philip taking the events very badly was sitting down trying to calm himself. Victoria and Elizabeth were with him. Victoria stood up and said to Robert, "Ok what do we do?"

Bill organised the coastguard giving the location of the boat, its four miscreants and the extent of their injuries. Victoria gathered everyone apart from Thomas, the African and the prostitute and seated them in the living area. She then joined Robert on the deck with the three. She asked Robert, "What are we to do with them?"

Robert suggested, "Take them to the harbour, and let them go on their own way. It would be up to them to ensure the African got medical attention and to steer clear of Baptiste and his friend's."

As they were docking Robert continued "I know how difficult this must be for you Victoria but you have to make your own decisions as hard as they might be."

Victoria replied, "I have already made my mind up, Philip needs my help and whatever circumstances Thomas may find himself in, they are of his own volition. Thomas will not accept help from us. We do not even know where he resides, the names of his friends or the places he visits. He knows we will help him, he does not even need to ask, but it is all thrown back in our faces. He blames us for everything and if I am not careful he will be the death of Philip."

Thomas listened to the conversation, not one to back down he left Victoria with this parting shot, "You are no mother, more interested in how you look and how your friends see you than your own children. What help have you ever given me, fuck-all?"

As they made their way off the boat Robert shouted

after Thomas, "While you are seeing to your friend's head the girl needs help as well."

Thomas turned to face Robert, "You fucking gorilla, bust his head open and then advise me on how to look after him. She just needs to get back on the street where we are heading, she will be okay."

Robert added, "Perhaps if you removed your sunglasses you would get a clearer picture of the world you live in."

Thomas had to have the last word, "I am not taking advice on my appearance from a moron, fuck you."

The three disappeared into the night.

Robert turned to Victoria, "She is not well, shivering and sweating all the signs of coming down off of drugs we need to check that cabin to make sure it's safe, no needles."

Victoria had a different agenda, "I thought you had left me/us Robert, I was terrified. I thought you had gone with your son. I would not have blamed you, no one would. Thomas called you a coward we know that is not true but we felt as if we were on our own. Forgive me for doubting you."

The ever-gracious Robert replied, "I would have thought the same."

Early next morning Robert received a call from Officer Grojean. They exchanged pleasantries but the officer had some worrying news for him. Baptiste and his merry band of men were not so merry. They had been active in this area for several months and had carried out several drug-related murders. The boat they were on was carrying approximately £500,000 worth of cocaine and their weapons of choice could now be matched to previous incidents. Grojean further explained that Baptiste had a penchant for behaving like a cowboy; that is drawing his gun and shooting on the move. The thing for Robert to consider was reprisal. Sometime in the future the Annabella would be spotted and who knew what might happen then?

Grojean added would Robert like to work for him? Robert declined the offer and thanked him for the information.

Chapter 9

20th of July 2006

The party was now settled back at the Villa. It was decided they would have several days rest before moving Philip and Alan. Victoria had spoken with the Hammersteins and they arranged for the boat to be put into dry dock. They were more concerned with how Philip was. There would always be boats but only one Philip.

Initially Alan was in some discomfort and much to his chagrin Josie was his personal nurse. As much as he complained at her constant fussing he healed in double quick time. Philip was more of a concern, the tremor in his hand had become worse and he really did not want to socialise with any one. When Robert approached Philip he seemed to turn his head away leading Robert to think that he blamed him. Victoria could see Philip's stance manifesting itself into a much greater problem, so she sat both men down together and told them to get on with it.

This may have been somewhat of an obstacle for talkative men but to Philip and Robert, who were both economical with words, it was a mountain to climb.

After several minutes of hand wringing and gut wrenching silence Philip blurted out, "I am so ashamed. Thomas was right it is not his shame it is my shame. Of all the people in the world I would not want to witness this debacle would be you. A man of honour and of courage who would not dream of sinking to such depths. I am truly sorry Robert that you had to be part of that farce."

Robert thought about his reply very carefully before saying, "Philip you know as well as I do we learn from our experiences but we move on. We have to, if we dwell on what has happened it will destroy us. The past is gone, over and done with unless we carry it with us. It will eat away at our very being until all that's left is bitterness. I do not see what Thomas did as a failing on your behalf I only need look at Elizabeth, all your friends and the staff you employ for affirmation as to what people think of you and the goodwill you wish for everyone. I really do not enjoy this sort of dialogue so let's put it behind us and move on."

Philip reached over gave Robert a hug and said to him, "Give me a hand getting outside, about time I showed my face."

21st of July 2006

Elizabeth came to Robert to apologise for her thoughtlessness and thank him for his help. Robert went straight to Victoria and said to her, "I'm really finding it quite difficult with the amount of people who are apologising and thanking me for my help. Stuff happens, we sort it out. I can't see the big deal."

Victoria continually amazed by Robert's innocence said, "If I did not know you better then I would think you were angling for something. For you there is no grey area, what you see is what you get. You see a problem you resolve it, if there are consequences you will solve them as well. The majority of people live in a very complex world, what happens if I do this, what will happen if I do that, what will she say what will he think and so on. If it were left to the people who think they know best Scarlett and myself would be God knows where Philip would have lost the will to live, Alan would have bled to death and Thomas et al would be suffering in one manner or another. There are very few people who would have dreamed of doing what you did let alone having the foresight and the ability to accomplish it. Take the apologies and the thanks. It is all we can do, you undertake the hard stuff, we stand back and thank God."

Later that day Robert again went to Victoria as he had some information for her. From his uneasy manner Victoria guessed that the information he was about to impart was to do with a woman. Knowing that no help was forthcoming from Victoria indeed she seemed to take a strange delight in seeing him struggle Robert blurted out, "Sandra is coming."

Victoria's face dropped, she replied, "Oh no, please tell me you are joking Robert."

Robert had known in his heart that Victoria would not like this news and her reaction confirmed his worst fears. Robert began to say, "I can only apologise for this unwelcome intrusion, I will call her."

Victoria interrupted him, her shoulders shaking with laughter "I am sorry Robert but I cannot keep this up.

Good, I am glad she is coming. I can meet the woman who once had Robert Green's heart, maybe I can learn a thing or two."

As she turned and walked away Robert could hear her muttering, "How should I wear my hair."

Robert thought to himself 'this is worse than I could ever imagine.'

22nd of July 2006

Robert and Luke met Sandra at the airport. Despite Robert's misgivings he was genuinely happy to see Sandra and even more satisfied with the positive effect she had on Luke. They were very close and for the next couple of days the three of them could behave like a proper family. Sandra had reserved a room for herself and Luke at a nearby hotel and on their way there they stopped at a local cafe for a drink. Sitting outside watching the people go by, soaking up the sun and just chatting when Scarlett, Elizabeth and Victoria came in and sat with them. Victoria explained that Elizabeth wanted her to see a shawl in one of the local shops. The three visitors would not stop for a drink as Victoria wanted to get back to the villa to check on Philip. Before they left Victoria spoke to Sandra whispering something in her ear. As they exited the cafe and walked along the street Victoria called out, "See you later, bye."

Luke disappeared inside the cafe to use the toilet. Sandra used this opportunity to quiz Robert, "Is that the Robert Green fan club?"

Caught unawares Robert said, "No."

Not to be deterred Sandra persisted, "Well Scarlett is obviously in love with you, Elizabeth I'm not sure and what is the story with Victoria?"

Robert, thinking to himself for gods sake hurry up Luke said, to Sandra, "There's no story."

Sandra pleased with herself that she had scored with a direct hit said to Robert, "I'll find out later on."

A perturbed Robert said, "What will you find out later on?"

Sandra mischievously tapped her nose.

An uneasy Robert returned to the villa a short while

later Victoria also returned carrying a shopping bag. Elizabeth and Scarlett were staying in town, making the most of what little time was left in France. Victoria asked Robert if he could spare a moment. Sitting in the coolest area of the villa eyes closed Philip sat listening to Rachmaninov. It was the first chance Robert had to scrutinise Philip. Despite the suntan he was saddened to see how much Philip had aged. Whether it was the illness, or the antics of Thomas, life was beginning to take its toll on the good man. Philip opened his eyes and said to Robert, "Sorry to drag you in here out of the sunshine but Victoria and I would value your opinion on a matter close to our hearts."

Robert made himself comfortable and said to Philip and Victoria, "Ok, I'm all ears."

Philip and Victoria out lined an idea that they had had for several years. They were desperate to help people wherever they could and they were in the fortunate position of having wealth land and property. Seeing how happy Luke was playing on the jet skis, dingy and fishing with Philip had really spurred them on to do something decisive. They were not saying that Luke needed help in any way shape or form but there were plenty of kids who did. So they were thinking of giving a chance of a holiday, a break from the hardship of life that some kids endured and maybe give a break to the parents as well.

Robert thought how many people in their position would have such **altruistic values. He said to both of them, "I think it is a fantastic idea, and any help you need with the setting up and running of it I would be only too happy to be involved. One thing though, what does Elizabeth think?"**

Victoria responded, "We are very pleased that you think it is a fantastic idea and even more pleased that you would like to be involved. You know that Elizabeth is going to university and that she will be studying social economics, well she feels that this will fit in with her studies. A working paper in progress so to speak."

Robert knew there would be a million things to sort out but there was one small matter that sprang to mind. Speaking openly to the Hawthorns he said, "I know you have plenty of money but a long-term project like this could be draining."

Philip reassured him, "There are several other families who want to be involved for instance the Hammersteins. Not necessarily hands-on but they would like their name to be associated with the venture. Of course we know that some people will use it as a publicity tool and really have no goodwill to any one but themselves but money is money and cannot be turned down." Philip paused for a moment before continuing, "Considering the mess Thomas is in this may seem a little ambitious and perhaps it is but we will do all we can for Thomas. He is in a privileged position, the children we want to help are not so fortunate."

Victoria stood up announcing that she had guests for the evening and time was of the essence. Philip and Robert sat for a while longer listening to the music. Robert wondered if there was more to this than met the eye. Robert was a little anxious.

Alan had been lucky in as much the crossbow bolt had failed to hit the bone and had only caused muscle damage. The main problem had been the material of his shirt. A small operation had been necessary to clear the material from causing any infection. He objected less and less to Josie's attention, resigned to the fact she actually cared for him and made a very good nurse.

As it was now, Josie was helping Victoria, Elizabeth and Scarlett make preparations for the evening while instructing Alan to sit down and relax.

At 7 p.m. Sandra arrived with Luke. Robert's former wife was silently proud of how everyone welcomed Luke. She mentioned this to Robert who informed her that the Hawthorns made every effort to treat everyone as they would wish to be treated. The evening passed pleasantly. They ate alfresco by the pool: the evening lights bouncing off the water reflecting into their eyes as if someone had sprinkled magic dust onto the happy people. Josie, Victoria, Sandra, Elizabeth and Scarlett danced to old Motown songs. Maybe because of the previous nightmare scenario and the sense of relief and safety and maybe just maybe a feeling of bonhomie swept over the happy people enticing Robert to join in with the dance.

Regardless of his elated emotions Robert could not help but notice how well Sandra and Victoria got on together. Sandra was cajoled into spending the night at the villa. Gone 2 a.m., Elizabeth and Scarlett were the last of the party to retire for the evening, peace and quiet descended on the villa.

23rd of July 2006

Early the next morning Sandra made her way to

the dining-room. Victoria was the only person present, eating toast and drinking coffee. Sandra asked that she might join her.

Victoria replied, "Sandra you do not have to ask, please treat this as your home while you are with us." Victoria added, "Another beautiful morning."

Sandra poured milk onto a small bowl of cereal and made herself a cup of tea. Sandra asked Victoria, "Where is everybody?"

Victoria between mouthfuls of toast said, "Philip is in bed, Josie has taken Alan a cup of tea, the girls are fast asleep, Robert and Luke are in the pool and here we are."

Sandra finished her cereal and started on a slice of toast. She looked at Victoria trying to sum her up. Deciding that her powers of reasoning must be on the wan she said to Victoria, "Forgive me for being blunt Victoria but there would seem to be a catch. You should be a family that moves in the higher echelons of society but here you are mixing, dare I say it, with us. What on earth do your friends say?"

Victoria smiled, she took a sip of coffee before replying, "You are quite right, there are many people who will not have anything to do with us. Our attitude to that is good riddance. Our true friends are a small select group of people who share our values and can be truly called friends. We enjoy our life, we enjoy people's company, we will help where we can. We think Robert, sorry we know Robert to have very similar values. You and Luke will always be welcome, just one thing Sandra, why did you and Robert go your separate ways?"

Sandra not expecting to be asked this question said, "An old cliché but true, another woman."

Victoria felt as if she had pried into an area where she should not have gone. She apologised for her clumsiness and hoped that Sandra did not think any less of her. It was just that Robert had never said anything.

Sandra, in an attempt to bring back harmony said, "I think it's me who needs to apologise Victoria, I may have misled you. The other woman was the army."

Victoria murmured, "Oh."

Sandra continued, "The Robert I left was completely

and totally wired into the SAS. Compared with the Robert that is relaxed and happy enough to dance. I am absolutely certain that the stories Luke told me about the boat are greatly exaggerated."

Victoria, relieved at not upsetting Sandra gave too much away in her answer, "No, I do not think so, he will have got his information from Robert. So if anything he has probably underplayed the drama. No, Robert was quite impressive, really magnificent."

Sandra collected her breakfast dishes together stood up leant towards Victoria and said, "I can see that." She continued, "if its okay with you may I swim for a while?"

Victoria blushing stuttered a response, "Of course, I am just going to check that Philip is okay."

Sandra and Luke left a short while later, Robert would collect them after lunch. Robert's plan had been to hire a car from one of the many car rental businesses situated in the town for a couple of days. That was until Philip and Victoria insisted that he took the jeep. Robert succumbed to their persuasion on the proviso that if there were to be a problem however slight they were to call him immediately any time of the day or night. He, Sandra and Luke were just going to drive down the coastline enjoying the views, playing on the beaches and soaking up the sun.

Before Robert left Victoria spoke to him through the driver's window of the jeep. "Sandra is in an attractive woman please do not fall in love with her again." Said through a breaking voice just managing to veil her emotions.

Robert realising how difficult Victoria was finding this quelled her fears, "If I think about it I never really loved Sandra, not then not now. We get along a lot better now than we ever did previously. We will both do the best for Luke and I will ensure that no harm comes to either of them. Please do not forget Victoria that a holiday is more conducive to people getting along better than the normal humdrum life most people endure. So, unless I receive a phone call I will see you tomorrow evening."

Ever conscious of other people's feelings they resisted the urge to kiss. Making do with a simple wave.

Sandra and Luke were waiting for Robert on the steps of the hotel. With just a small amount of luggage to load into the back of the jeep they were quickly on the road. They drove for approximately three quarters of an hour before stopping at a small cafe that led down to the beach. Luke had a fizzy drink and then ran down to the water's edge to play. From their elevated position Robert and Sandra could see that Luke was safe. Sandra chose her moment to say to Robert, "Wonderful people, the Hawthorns. Not at all what I expected, kind and considerate. You can see that from the way they treat Josie and Alan."

Robert treading carefully responded, "Yes they are, doesn't feel like work. I guess that's the way they intended it to be."

Sandra, "And Victoria, stunning. You would think with her looks and her money she would be up her own arse."

Robert thinking long and hard to himself wondered if Sandra was trying to provoke an argument or if she was just trying to gauge his reactions.

Robert replied, "Has Victoria said something to you?"

"No." said Sandra. She continued, "Honestly it is so obvious. I only wonder what Philip makes of it. I've only known Victoria for a very short period of time but she's a woman of principles and knowing you as I do you have the same principles. Do not misunderstand me Robert. I like Victoria and at this moment in time right here right now I like you as well. You are a changed man Robert relaxed, chatty and interested. I sincerely hope that it all works out for the both of you."

Robert said to Sandra, "Thank you, it means a lot."

Sandra could see that Luke was making his way back up said to Robert, "I'll tell you one thing. Philip and Victoria, there's no sex going on and hasn't been for some time."

Robert wondered how on earth she had come to that conclusion.

The trio spent a very pleasant couple of days together. No heroics required, none asked for. Sandra did not ask Robert about his exploits on the Annabella. She knew that he would not be too forthcoming with any information and frankly all of that macho behaviour was, thank God, in the past. Of course it was a different matter when it came to looking after Luke but men squaring up to each other turned her stomach.

On the Monday evening they drove back to the hotel where Sandra and Luke were staying. A car was hired for mother and son so that the rest of the coastline could be explored for the remainder of the week. They agreed to one last visit to the villa in order to say goodbye to the Hawthorns and staff. Philip gave Luke a small momento, Robert issued the usual warnings about being careful and to call him if there were a problem and Victoria made Sandra promise that she would visit them.

Chapter 10

29th of July 2006

The following weekend back at the Hawthorns house life continued more or less as usual. Alan was told there was no need to come in and to take as much rest as he needed but Alan did come in and usually at the same time as Josie. As much as the rest of the staff wanted to fuss over Alan and ask questions, Josie fended them off as if Alan were her own personal property.

Victoria spoke to Robert regarding Philip, "I am worried. Philip has no interest in anything whatsoever. He has not mentioned the holiday camp for the kids, talked about Thomas or spoken to Elizabeth regarding university. The weather is good but he will not sit out for any length of time preferring to stay in the library reading about world affairs in the papers. The only thing I can think of is the M.S. He is quite unsteady on his feet now, maybe it is getting to him. Would you try talking to him Robert?"

"Yes" Robert replied, "but not by myself. Philip is too shrewd a man to know when people have been talking about him. We will go and see him now and see if we can get to the root of this problem."

Philip was in the library, head buried in the morning's paper. A small fan was blowing directly at Philip. He looked up as Victoria and Robert entered the room.

"This looks serious." Said Philip.

"We are worried" replied Victoria.

Philip studied Robert and Victoria before replying, "And what is it you have to worry about dear?"

The use of 'dear' put Victoria on the attack. She responded angrily, "Who the hell do you think you are calling me dear? Do not dare to patronise me Philip. I want to help you. If there is something bothering you then let me know so that we can resolve whatever is the problem."

A thoroughly chastened Philip apologised to Victoria and went on to say, "There is so much to do and I have no energy and who knows how much time left."

Robert spoke up, "Philip you have been helping other folk for years. Don't you think it's about time you gave the chance to let people repay that kindness? Others want to help, it's not a case of asking just say what you need and what you want done and we will do our best. Any one who knows you will understand your situation and will gladly undertake any task put to them. As for how much time left I cannot believe you are talking like that. So what is first Philip?"

Begrudgingly Philip agreed and for the rest of the day the three of them worked on plans for the holiday camp. Philip, initially a reluctant participant, soon became the fulcrum. The list of people to contact who could possibly help grew and grew. Council officers, banks, architects, charitable organisations, building firms and on it went. Not just names, personal contacts that at one time or another Philip had done business with. They also drew up a schedule for how much time could be allocated to the project on a daily basis. Bearing in mind there was still a need to manage the estate, Philip's physiotherapy and his rest periods. Or as he liked to call it, his downtime.

Philip suggested that maybe Robert would like to become more involved in the running of the estate. Of course it was entirely up to Robert but it might be interesting. Robert agreed there and then, he more or less already knew the running of the estate. Organisation was the order of the day.

Robert turned down the invite to stay for dinner and left early evening. He made his way out of the back door and was walking across the yard when he heard Victoria calling him. He turned to see her approach him. She was wearing the clothes that she had worn all day but he just noticed how beautiful she was. A pair of trainers, fairly tight jeans and a white blouse showing a small amount of cleavage. She could have been wearing old sackcloth she would still look beautiful. Standing in front of him she said, "What are you looking at?"

Robert composed his thoughts, he hoped that she had not caught him looking at her body. Finally he uttered, "I'm not looking at anything, I was just wondering what you wanted?"

Victoria gave him a look that said I do not believe you and she said, "I will walk with you a little way to the gatehouse."

Once out of the yard Victoria said to Robert, "Do you think Philip will be ok?"

"There is no way of knowing what the disease will do next. What I do know is that Philip needs to be kept occupied, to feel he is being useful. The project will keep his spirits up." said Robert.

Victoria agreed and said to Robert, "You are ok with the extra responsibility? Remember we would also like you to be involved with the running of the project."

The ex-SAS man mulled it over in his mind for a moment or two then he said, "This whole estate runs like clockwork if the same efficiency is applied to the project then there is not a problem. I am only too glad to be of help and I consider it an honour that you have asked me."

"Good" said Lady Hawthorn "now tell me what you

were looking at in the yard?"

"If I told you I was thinking that the fencing needed work, you would know I was lying. The truth is I was looking at you Victoria." Robert admitted.

"Glad to hear it. Hope you like what you see? Now tell me what is this I hear about you and Scarlett?"

Robert, "Yes I definitely like what I see. Me and Scarlett, I don't follow?"

Victoria, "I will make this easier for you Robert. Last Saturday evening at the villa, in the small hours, you had a visit. Should I go on or would you care to elucidate?"

Robert, "I guess this information has come via Elizabeth. Yes I had a visit from Scarlett."

Victoria growing impatient, "Bloody hell Robert, and……?"

Robert, "I said nothing to save the girl's blushes. She came into my room, wearing next to nothing and was quite clear about her intentions. I refused her as gently as I could. Scarlett was in my company for four or five minutes. She left the room, went outside and sat next to the pool for a little while. She came back to the villa and disappeared into her room. When I was happy that she was safe and secure I went back to bed. Have I left anything out?"

Victoria, "I believe you Robert but Scarlett has a slightly different version. I suppose she does not want to lose face in front of her friends. Does sex not bother you Robert, I think I can safely say most men would have welcomed Scarlett's advances?"

They had reached the halfway point between the house and the gatehouse. It was turning into a beautiful evening, the warmth of the day wrapped itself around the two protagonists endeavouring to move them closer and the sky took on a golden hue ready to crown their moment. It was all to no avail not even the forces of nature could undermine Robert's and Victoria's determination not to let it happen.

They could not and would not deceive Philip.

Robert at long last answered, "Scarlett is an attractive young woman in mind and body but she is not for me. You bother me Victoria and if that includes sex then yes it bothers me. I will see you tomorrow. Goodbye."

Robert continued on his way, in the distance he could just about hear the quad, Philip out with the dogs. Looking to his left, in the far distance he could make out Elizabeth on her favoured horse, Meadow, making her way back to the stables. To his right the parched river ran gently barely splashing the stones that broke it's run. The grass cutters had been out that day and the smell of a fresh cut lawn was powerful. Life went on.

Robert entered the gatehouse. He knelt in front of his CD collection, selecting a soul compilation that Sandra had bought for him. He inserted the disk into the player and let the music take its course. Usually soul mellowed his thoughts and gave him a clearer vision, the lead vocalist in perfect harmony with the music. Not tonight, he turned the music up loud so that he could hear it wherever he was in the house. Next he went into the kitchen to have his evening meal, pasta, fried bacon, peppers, onions and mushrooms. The music and the food did nothing to relax him or satisfy his appetite.

Pouring a scotch for himself he sat back on his old leather chair, although it had been with him for several years he had only begun to use it since he left the army.

Whatever Robert did, wherever he moved Victoria moved with him. He could not shake her from his thoughts, he did not want to.

9:30 a.m. 30th of July 2006

Robert spoke to Luke via the PC. They had set it up so as well as talking they could see one another. Robert asked Luke how the rest of the holiday had been.

Luke answered, "Good, would have been better if you'd been there dad. Guess what Philip gave me?"

Robert thought about the small package and could only guess, "A dead bullet."

Luke eager to tell his dad said, "A lions claw."

Robert was suitably impressed.

Luke continued, "He put a note in with it. Shall I read it to you dad?"

Robert said, "Yes."

Luke read from a piece of paper he was holding in

his hand,

"Dear Luke,

Here is a lion's claw.

Given to me by The Chief of an African tribe known as the Bachokwe, located in Zaire.

The Chief's name Mr Fred, well that was what he called himself.

The story goes, while out hunting Mr Fred was attacked by a huge lion. Bearing in mind these people are descended from pygmies. Two of the tribe managed to overpower and kill the beast. The claw was buried in Mr Fred's leg. It is a symbol of great courage.

Have to go now

Yours sincerely

Philip.

Robert said, "Very good, Mr Fred hey, bet he was an interesting character."

Luke added, "I think its Mr Fred, the writing keeps changing."

Robert asked Luke to hold the piece of paper up to the camera. After viewing the paper Robert asked Luke, "Would you like to thank Philip?"

Luke said yes he would. Robert asked after Luke's mum, she was standing nearby and spoke with Robert for a little while. They set up a time that would be convenient to Luke and Philip. After the call Robert wondered how Philip had come to have the claw and also if Victoria had noticed even writing a few simple lines caused Philip to struggle.

10:30 a.m.

Another hot day Robert thought as he made his way up to Hawthorn Hall to see Philip. Josie told Robert that Lord Hawthorn was in the dining room. The door wide open, Robert made himself known before entering. Victoria was with her husband, without looking she asked if Robert would mind giving them a hand. Philip wanted to sit by the window and was having a problem getting to his feet. Once the older man was sitting comfortably, shaded from the sun Robert said, "Shall I go ahead and do your rounds for you?"

Victoria answered for her husband, "Yes, could you. Also the hardware store in the village sells walking sticks would you mind popping along tomorrow and purchasing one?"

Philip spoke up, "No, I will get my own walking stick."

Robert agreed and said that he would take Philip to try them out. Philip asked for a fan to be positioned so that he could benefit from cool air blowing at his head. This done Robert went about his morning's work.

The former SAS man had got to the end of his round when Victoria attracted his attention. She was wearing jodhpurs, black leather boots up to her knees and a figure hugging white T-shirt. Robert could not help but notice how well proportioned she was.

He said to her, "I am surprised you have been out on the horse, it is a little warm for that."

Victoria replied, "No, I have been helping Elizabeth in the stable. We have friends visiting this afternoon and if it's cool enough they will take the horses out."

Robert asked Victoria, "What is Philip's connection with Africa in particular Zaire?"

Victoria gave Robert an abrupt answer, "Ask Philip."

Not to be put off from more urgent matters Robert mentioned to Victoria the note Philip had written to Luke, in regard to Phillip's handwriting, did she think his deterioration was a little too rapid. Victoria considered this for a moment before answering, "I keep in regular touch with our consultant friend in fact he is coming along next weekend. The truth of the matter is there is no way of knowing. There are too many variables, the heat although he was fine on the boat he struggles here, having to deal with Thomas undoubtedly sets him back and his age. The physiotherapist will now come twice a week instead of once, and even then she says it may be too much for him. I work with him every morning but I really am at a loss as to what to do next. What he could do last Monday he will not be able to do this Monday. This illnesses is terrible. The insidious manner in which it takes over the body to see someone you love dearly deteriorate in front of your eyes can be too much to bear, but it cannot be so, however bad it is for the onlooker it is a damn-sight worse for the afflicted individual."

"I know you are in the front line and that is a very lonely place to be, but you do know the amount of support and goodwill people give you."

Robert started his considered response he continued, "Never forget Victoria we will do whatever we can to help."

Victoria said, "Thank you. About last night."

Robert cut her off immediately, "No more Victoria, look after your husband."

The next morning Robert collected Philip and they went into the village. The hardware shop owner, Mr Brigsby, was delighted to see Philip and called Mrs Brigsby. The insistent wife made them all a cup of tea and presented a homemade cake, apple and blueberry. After tasting the delicious offering Robert asked her if she sold the cakes. Mrs Brigsby threw her arms up in horror, "Sold, for goodness sake what is the world coming to."

She disappeared into the back of the shop still admonishing Robert. The stout Mrs Brigsby returned still incredulous at the youth of today. She handed Robert a carrier bag containing two more cakes with the instructions, "When you have finished these come back to me I will put some meat on your bones and don't bring any money."

Meanwhile Philip and Mr Brigsby were selecting a stick.

After much deliberation Philip chose a burned and polished ash type. Philip said, "Beautiful, fits the hand perfectly."

Robert could see the benefit at once. Philip managed to get to the car by himself. On the return home Robert asked Philip, "Do I resemble a thin youth?".

A laughing Philip responded, "Well, compared to

Mrs Brigsby. 'There is more meat on a butcher's pencil' to coin a phrase. Let me ask you a question, how old you think Mrs Brigsby is?"

Robert pondered, "Mmmm I guess between 55 and 60."

"You would be guessing wrong. Mrs Brigsby is at least 70 and anyone under 50 she considers a youth."

Robert let out a whistle before replying, "Impressive, so that would put Mr Brigsby at approximately the same age. I wonder what their secret is and how come you received no cake?"

Philip, "Their secret, pure speculation old boy. Sound genes, fresh vegetables, fruit, meat and good old-fashioned home cooking. If I were to take a home baked cake into Hawthorn Hall a civil war would ensue. The kitchen against Mrs Brigsby, toss a coin for the outcome."

Robert smiled at the thought of anyone taking on

Mrs Brigsby. His thoughts were interrupted by Philip saying, "I have said to you before Robert do not isolate yourself from the village. They are good folk, get to know them and a word of warning. Mrs Brigsby will be expecting you do not let her down."

Robert's thoughts turned to Africa. Had Philip a dark secret. His mobile rang. It was Jim. When he had finished the call Philip asked if everything was okay?

Robert said, "Jim is coming up at the weekend wants to talk."

Maybe this will be a chance to put your plan into action and meet the villagers."

Over the coming days Robert saw as much of Victoria as he usually did. But they did not make any attempt to speak with one another as they had been. The following weekend all parties would be kept busy with guests.

8 p.m. Friday 4th August 2006

Jim arrived by taxi. He had elected to travel by train and get a cab from the station. It was good to see his friend again in more relaxed circumstances and not to be asking favours in pressure situations. They had something to eat and went along to the Badger for the last hour. Robert asked his friend, "What was it specifically you wanted to talk about?"

A despondent Jim replied, "She's gone."

Robert, "I take it you mean Melanie has left you."

"Yeah" Jim went on to explain, "She's been seeing someone else, uprooted the kids and moved in with him. Strange that, I can usually spot a hair out of place but when my wife's been shagged under my nose I can't see it. The police force is littered with divorcees. Once you're in uniform the job takes precedence over everything else. In fact the only thing that stopped me from finding the bastard and belting him was the effect it would have on my job."

Robert felt for his friend, thinking back to his own break-up with Sandra it's just not easy. Although there was not a lot of love between him and Sandra you always had to do the right thing for the child or children in Jim's case.

"How long has she been gone?" enquired Robert.

"A few weeks" Jim reflected, "if I look at it logically, it's for the best, phone calls in the middle of the night, don't worry your calls were one of dozens, seven days a week and night's if they thought they could get away with it. I know my colleagues better than my wife."

Jim got up to use the toilet when he sat back down he said to Robert, "There's a bit of a do tomorrow night at the village hall fancy going?"

"Yes" responded Robert, "why not, I have not been out for God knows how long."

"You never know we might get lucky." said a hopeful Jim.

The next morning Jim went along with Robert to see Philip and Victoria. Robert left Jim chatting with the Hawthorns while he went about his work. When he returned he found all of them plus Elizabeth sitting in the drawing-room drinking tea. As soon as he went through the door Victoria said to him, "Out tonight, are you looking for local talent?"

Philip told her that he disapproved of using such crass language.

As they walked back down to the gatehouse Jim said to Robert, "I know Philip is a good man and he has that terrible illness to contend with but you must feel something for Victoria."

Robert confided in Jim, by the time he had finished the tale they were sitting on the riverbank fishing.

Jim did not answer until they were leaving the river. "I'm not sure what you want to do about it Robert, you have changed calmer, more relaxed and what does that mean. To all intents and purpose you are happier, the job you are performing suits you. The people like you and you like the people. A lot of folks would think this paradise. Do you need a woman in your life to complete the idyll? Personally speaking I just need someone to fuck with, a night of passion. That will be proof enough for me I'm still alive and kicking but you are different. Maybe you have found what you're looking for but it is just unattainable. Of course saying that to an ex-SAS man is not strictly true is it?

You're not planning on taking Hawthorn Hall by force are you?"

The last comment was said with humour intended.

Robert smiled and said, "I wish I hadn't said anything, you useless bastard. I've got more questions than answers. Mind you going out in a blaze of glory? Na, too much trouble. Let's have a beer, something to eat and get a taxi into the village."

The two friends called into the Badger first. The pub

was packed. Robert asked the landlord what the occasion was.

"This is the last dance before Christmas" the landlord answered, he continued, "People just want to let their hair down."

Robert returned with the drinks, Guinness for Robert and the guest ale for Jim. His friend was wasting no time, chatting to a couple of women. Robert joined in with their convivial chat. They were going to the dance and said they would see them in there. Jim finished off his pint and went to get another round. At 10 p.m. the two men went over to the village hall. The dance was in full swing and everyone was having a good time. Robert could not believe his eyes when he saw the DJ introduce the next record, Nirvana Smells Like Teen Spirit. Mr Brigsby of all people. When the next slow song came on, The Streets - Dry Your Eyes Mate, a woman asked Robert for a dance, then another and another. The last woman he danced with told Robert that she was a friend of the woman who was currently sticking her tongue down Jim's throat. Robert quite liked Stephanie and offered to share a taxi home with her. Stephanie replied, "I think that is already organised."

At the end of the dance Robert, Stephanie, Jim and Ruth met outside. They found a taxi and went back to the gatehouse. They were only inside for 10 minutes when Jim and Ruth disappeared upstairs. Robert and Stephanie stared at each other listening to the noise coming from upstairs. Robert said to Stephanie, "Your friend sounds like a virgin."

Stephanie gave a one-word answer, "Hardly."

Robert, "What does that mean?"

Stephanie, "She has three kids, oh yeah and she's married."

Robert, "Oh fuck!" He reconciled himself to the problems that would incur."

Stephanie's next question took Robert by surprise. "Do you fancy a bit of wrestling?" she said staring at the ceiling. Robert answered, "Thanks for the offer but I'll give it a miss."

"Thought you might. You don't look the type." Stephanie mysteriously answered. She continued, "Do you mind if I go up?"

Robert asked her, "I don't suppose you mean to go to bed do you?"

The spirited Stephanie said, "Sort of, he is rather delicious."

With that the lively woman went upstairs. Robert decided to sleep outside in the peace and quiet with only the sound of the leaves and running water to keep him company. Plus of course his thoughts of Victoria, always Victoria.

Sunday 6th August 2006

At 8 a.m. Robert returning from his morning run spotted Jim near the riverbank working with weights.

"Didn't think you would have the energy for that?" Robert teased.

"You would be surprised at what energy I have got. I've half a mind to go upstairs and start all over again." came back Jim's retort.

Robert's heart sank, "I take it they're still here?"

Jim, feeling the first pangs of regret said, "'Fraid so. I'll get them up you arrange a taxi."

"No" replied Robert, "every gossip in the village will know they've been here if they get a taxi. You get them up I'll get a car." Before going up to Hawthorn Hall Robert pulled on a vest. Although it was still early, he did not want to bump in to anyone half naked.

For once Robert let himself in through the kitchen door without his customary knock, only to surprise Alan and Josie in a clinch. Robert thought to himself, fuck me the whole world is at it. Once the culinary staff had disentangled themselves he said to Alan, "I need the car for 20 minutes, need something from the village, I can be reached on my mobile."

Alan was just going to say that Victoria was in the drawing room but Robert was gone. Alan hurried through to the drawing room and relayed Robert's message to Victoria. She dashed out of the drawing room, out the front door and down the steps just as Robert came round the corner. She flagged him down and climbed into the front passenger seat.

"You are in a hurry." Victoria observed that Robert's

vest clung to his sweat drenched body.

Robert composed himself and measured his response very carefully, "No, I'm not really. Where would you like to go?"

Victoria responded, "Same place as you, the village. Something has happened to the village hall." The lady eyed Robert suspiciously.

Robert considered his options, drive past the waiting party or collect them. Driving past was a non-starter it basically said look at who I was fucking last night.

As Robert approached the gatehouse he could see the happy campers waiting on the drive, there was another option. Run the fucker's down. Robert could not bring himself to look at the women but was aware that they were half dressed. He did not open his window so Jim went round to Victoria's side.

"Another beautiful day." He heard the jovial policeman say. The two women, after some effort got in the back. As soon as the doors closed Robert pulled away leaving Jim in midsentence, seemingly oblivious to the discomfort he was causing Robert.

Now all he had to hope for was that Ruth and Stephanie would keep their mouths closed. Ruth soon put paid to any hope of silence. "Is this yours Bob?" her opening salvo.

"No." Robert decided that to keep the conversation to an absolute bare minimum. Damage limitation and who the hell called him Bob.

"Is it okay to have a cigarette Bob?"

"No." replied Robert.

"Fuck you then." came the response.

Robert tried to steal a glance at Victoria but he could not tell if she were amused or not. He heard Stephanie and Ruth discuss Victoria. To be fair to Stephanie she did try to whisper.

"I think that is Lady Hawthorn." Stephanie said.

"Lady Fucking Bollocks." was Ruth's considered reply.

"No, I definitely think it is Lady Hawthorn." persisted

the whispering Stephanie.

Ruth who obviously did not care for anyone or anyone's status said, "You should have joined in last night Bob, could have done with another bloke or is one woman enough for you."

Victoria said to the ashen-faced Robert, "Slow down."

Robert did not bother answering the last question. He pulled over. "Right, you two out." he roared at the two startled women.

Robert got out of the car and helped the two reluctant passengers on their way. A dismayed Ruth said, "Fucking hell mate, you aren't half rough for a gay."

The two women wandered off down a lane. Robert and Victoria preceded into the village. Robert calmly said, "Where in the village do you want to go to Victoria?" belying his seething rage.

An also raging Victoria responded, "The village hall, a place you are quite familiar with Bob." She deliberately over pronounced Bob.

Robert pulled up outside of what was left of the village hall, Victoria said to Robert, "You had better come with me."

There were several people outside the burnt ruins of the village hall. One of them addressed Victoria, "Lady Hawthorn, this is very kind of you to come out on such short notice. We won't go in, it could be dangerous but our immediate concerns are the Harvest Festival and a week of Christmas school plays."

Victoria introduced Robert. The official, John Trout who had spoken to Victoria said, "I know Mr Green, well I have seen him about with Lord Hawthorn."

Robert said to John Trout, "I thought the church organised the Harvest Festival?"

"It does normally but there was some damage done in the church during the week, quite substantial damage and it was decided to switch the Harvest Festival to the hall, but alas." John Trout made a sweeping gesture with his arm encompassing the entire hall.

Victoria asked, "Any idea how it happened?"

"It's only guesswork at the moment but we think maybe there were a couple doing what they should not be doing in the store room." said a John Trout, trying to be as polite as he possibly could.

Victoria put a question to Robert, "What do you think Robert?"

Caught off guard Robert replied, "About how the fire started?"

Victoria stepped closer to Robert, "No, is that all you can think of." stepping back from Robert she said in a louder voice, "The Harvest Festival we can rearrange without a problem, the school plays could be a little more awkward. Robert can you find out the details please."

For the best part of the next hour Robert dealt with the people who ran the village hall. By the end he felt it would be possible but he had to check one or two dimensions. He took Mrs Rawlings' number and said he would get back to her.

The tension in the car on the drive back was palpable, Robert tried to apologise to Victoria but she was having none of it.

Eventually she spoke, "I can understand your frustrations. Your loyalty to Philip is undeniable. But to sleep with a pair of sluts and then wave them under my nose and to add insult to injury to be called Lady Fucking Bollocks in my own car while giving a lift to the sluts is unforgivable. How could you Robert? Do you think I do not get frustrated, do you think that over the years I have not had propositions. Stop the car."

The car came to a halt. Victoria turned and looked directly into Robert's eyes. She sat silent for a while before admitting, "The last time I had sex was the night Elizabeth was conceived. Philip just does not like sex, he put up with the act for the sake of procreation. Not because he is not man enough and not because he was not able, he just does not like sex. I have tried a thousand times to talk to him about it but he just shuts down. Do you know what that does for your self-esteem? Do you know what it feels like for the person you love to reject you for 22 long years? Do you know what it feels like to have countless people tell you how beautiful you are, how stunning you look? Well let me tell you Bob, it does not matter how you look when the person you are with does not want you. But you have a solution don't you Bob, fuck the first thing that comes along. I thought you were different. How could you Robert, how could you?"

By now Victoria was in floods of tears, only just managing to

spit out the last bitter words of betrayal from her mouth.

Robert started the car, he raced the last couple of miles to the gates of Hawthorn Hall skidding to a halt outside the gatehouse, sending clouds of dust from the gravel drive into the arid air. Robert ordered Victoria to go with him. Inside the house Jim was sitting in Robert's chair, feet up enjoying a cup of coffee and a slice of toast. One look at Robert and Victoria told him all was not well.

He decided to stand. Placing his mug on the floor and looking for somewhere to put his unfinished toast, he turned to face the clandestine couple. Robert demanded that he told Victoria what had transpired the previous evening. Jim related the tale to Victoria concluding with, "and Robert slept outside."

Victoria quickly looked at Robert then said to Jim, "What about Melanie?"

Jim matter-of-factly said, "Oh that's over."

Victoria, "I am sorry to hear that. Is there any chance of reconciliation?" She added, "I hope you are being sensible and using protection."

Jim, "Na, she's already shacked up with someone else. Don't worry about me Vicki, first rule of combat is always protect yourself."

Robert could not believe his ears, "For fuck's sake" he exclaimed, "what is this? A health and safety meeting for sex addicts? Vicki, where the fuck did you get Vicki from?"

Jim interrupted, "Mind your language Robert there is a lady present."

Robert speaking directly to Victoria, "You were in pieces a moment ago."

Victoria, "I know, but I do not like to hear of people splitting up."

Robert was dumbfounded all he could say was, "Clean your face and I will give you a lift back up to the house."

Back in the car Victoria said to Robert, "I hope Jim will be ok."

Robert responded, "Stop worrying about Jim, he will be fine. I am more worried about us Victoria."

"No need to" Victoria reassured him, "we know the rules and as hard as they are to follow, we will. I should not have told you about Philip, that was a mistake but in the heat of the moment. Yet again I doubted you and once again you proved yourself unimpeachable, I am sorry Robert." Then to herself, "They were real sluts."

As they got out of the car Robert said that he was going to do his work and he would be in the next morning to measure the hall.

Robert could not stay mad at Jim, he was like a kid in a sweet shop and just grabbed a handful. They parted that evening still the best of friends.

Monday 07th August 2006

Robert was in the hall, known as 'The Great Hall' when Philip and Victoria came in. He noticed how much Philip was struggling to walk. He was using his stick, Victoria helping keep him steady. He seemed to be deteriorating daily.

Robert said to the Hawthorns, "Good morning, how was your weekend?"

Victoria answered, "Frank (Dr Kneebone) and Charlotte are good friends and good company, we had a pleasant weekend."

Robert detected a reticence to elaborate so he decided to ask Victoria at a later time, Philip was very quiet. Sticking to the business in hand Robert said, "I can see that the hall is more than adequate but to be on the safe side I will measure it."

Philip piped up, "I have drawings, they are in the library."

Robert went to fetch the drawings, he returned a short while later carrying the relevant documents.

"That is quite a collection you have." Robert said to Philip. He continued, "I take it these are not the originals?" adding, "Is it ok to lie this on the floor?"

A newly invigorated Philip said, "By all means, just lay them down by your feet. These are copies, the originals are in a museum, in London. Copy drawings for the whole of the house are in the library. It really is a comprehensive collection, not just the building, interior and the various features you see dotted around the gardens."

The rest of the morning was taken up with not just the Great Hall drawing but looking at the various sketches available. Robert was surprised to find three secret rooms woven into the main structure.

Robert informed Philip and Victoria that he had contacted the fire service and they were coming to see him on Thursday morning also he would be in touch with the police.

Philip wondered why the police needed to be involved and said to Robert, "While the fire service is here ask them to check the whole house but why are you getting the police involved?"

Robert responded, "The school plays are not a problem but I was out in the village on Saturday night and there seemed to be a few undesirables floating about and of course the church was damaged."

"I do not know about the undesirables but the village folk have always struck me as a decent crowd. Must be outsiders." Philip replied.

"Yes, I would agree with that. Any idea who the undesirables are?" Victoria chimed in.

Robert acutely aware that Victoria was talking to him said, "Not really, just some fellows hanging around the pub."

Phillip said to Victoria, "Robert knows best so leave him be. Come on, we will have a spot of lunch and then I will have a nap. Fancy something to eat Robert?"

"No thank you." replied the former soldier.

Over the next few weeks Philip and Robert were involved in several meetings regarding the setting up of the holiday camp. Robert was also involved with Victoria in organising the harvest festival. The long-range weather forecast indicated a dry day but to be on the safe side it could be moved into the Great Hall if required.

Sunday 17th September 2006

The day started with a burst of energy. The sun shone on the people who set up the offerings. By midday it was quiet again. Only a few people remained. The Hawthorns, a few of the kitchen staff and some of the farm hands who had helped with lifting and carrying. Scarlett was also present, she had spent the weekend with Elizabeth and was more than happy to be involved with the harvest festival. At an opportune moment Scarlett spoke to Robert, "I feel I need to apologise to you Robert, I made a fool of myself the last time we were together." Robert confused by her choice of words responded, "There really is no need to apologise, blame it on the alcohol."

Scarlett took another stab at kindling a romance, "Perhaps if I had not been so forward, approached you in a more subtle manner."

Robert feeling a little uncomfortable at Scarlett's persistent advances said, Scarlett, you are obviously an attractive young woman and there is the problem, you are too young."

Scarlett, not to be deterred, "I maybe young but I am experienced, both ways, ask Elizabeth."

Robert was not that naive that he did not know what

both ways meant and now he knew about Elizabeth's sexuality. Robert thought to himself, today started so well.

"Scarlett, I do not wish to know about yours or any one else's sexuality. Please leave it be." The spurned young woman relented but not without a last word, "Ok, I get the picture. But do not think I have given up."

Robert resigned himself to the fact that she would be back and God knows what she is saying to Elizabeth.

Sunday 17th September 2006 2p.m.

A good number of people gathered at the Hawthorns estate. As the afternoon drew on the heat increased. What started out as a very pleasant sunny day rapidly turned into a humid, uncomfortable afternoon. It became too much for Philip, he disappeared inside, comfort found in the cool and the shade. By 4 p.m. people began to drift off wilting under the heat only to be replaced by a different crowd. Robert was chatting to a single mother, Jeanette, they were getting along rather well when she said, "The people who have just arrived are a bad lot, so I'm going to grab Jenny and get going. If I give you my number it's up to you whether you get in touch or not."

Victoria came to Robert, "What is wrong he asked her?"

"The two sluts we gave a lift to are back and they are with a very unpleasant crowd of men." Victoria replied.

"Do you see the runt" Robert nodded, "he put his hand inside my blouse and said to his friends, "The lady has brought a nice pair of melons for the harvest" Of course that was greeted with howls of laughter."

Robert responded, "Ok, there are only a few of us here so get every everyone inside and lock the doors. Do not bother bringing any thing with you, just get yourselves inside."

Victoria became worried, "There is only you here Robert, all the farm hands have gone, be careful."

After a few minutes when he was sure that everyone that mattered was safely inside Robert approached the gang of men plus the two women.

Overhead the clouds gathered and darkened, if it were possible the humidity seem to increase.

Ruth was the first to speak, "Here he is, Mr gay 2006."

More laughter.

Robert spoke calmly to the rabble, "Could you please leave?"

One of the men mimicked Robert, "Could you please fuck off?" but said with camp overtones.

Yet again shrieks of laughter greeted this comment. Robert stared at the runt. The insignificant piece of human dross felt intimidated and backed into the safety of the pack.

A bigger and more confident thug stepped forward, "You got a problem queer?" he barked. No laughter.

It became very dark, the thunder rumbled and lightning fizzed across the black sky. If there was one thing Robert did not have at that moment in time was a problem. Five men and two women, all of them under the influence of drink. One man had stepped forward, the other four would only join in if their friend was winning.

The thug edged forward towards Robert. They stood nose to nose. The thug reeked of alcohol and stale cigarettes, he breathed hatred into Robert's face.

The heavens opened and the rain fell towards the ground in fist size drops.

The thug stepped back and swung a punch, aimed at Robert's head. Anticipating his move Robert punched the thug in the stomach. Because of his backward movement, the swinging of a fist and the punch to the stomach the thug was caught off balance. Moving forward Robert kicked the thug in the bollocks, the man doubled over, he then pulled the would-be attackers head downwards onto his knee breaking his nose.

Not finished Robert turned to the others and landed a haymaker on the side of the runt's face.

Ruth screamed out, "We'll have the law onto you."

Robert replied matter-of-factly, "Your friends will enjoy that. Local hard man beaten up by a gay man."

The wretched gang, soaked to the skin made their way back to the van they had arrived in and drove off.

Robert returned to the house, Philip was in the process of getting up and had missed all the action, the storm had awoken him.

Robert said to Victoria, "Can you call the police and inform them that we have had a small incident, really to find out who these people are."

The next morning when Robert had finished his round Victoria said to him, "I spoke to the police. Seems that the people you encountered yesterday have gone. They had upset quite a few people in the village and in return were getting grief, you must have been the straw that broke the camel's back."

"I see you were getting on rather well with one of the village ladies yesterday." Victoria pointed out to Robert.

"Yes" he responded.

Victoria stared at Robert and said, "You know I want to know, yes will not suffice."

Robert had a question for Victoria, "Are you jealous?"

Victoria becoming irritable, no answer forthcoming and being asked questions she responded, "Good god, why is it always so difficult to get an answer from you."

Robert did answer, "She gave me her phone number and told me to call her, if I wanted to. Also would you like to know what Scarlett proposed?"

Victoria, visibly angered, turned heel and walked off in a huff. Without knowing it Robert had the upper hand in their non-physical relationship. Sometime later Victoria said to Robert, "Did you call her?"

"Yes." he replied.

Trying to keep her temper under control Victoria urged Robert to tell her what was going on.

Robert could not understand Victoria's inquisitiveness and so as not to rile the good lady he said to her, "I have rung her, her name is Jeanette by the way, but no date is arranged. Before you ask, I do like her and I suppose that a date could have been arranged. But where would that leave me? Precisely nowhere because I would always be looking behind me to see where you were. Which would be unfair to Jeanette, unfair to me and may be unfair to you. So there you have it. Happy?"

September dragged its heels in to October and came with a cold snap. Everyone in his family and employed by him hoped this would suit Philip and improve his well-being. Unfortunately fatigue still plagued him and now poor circulation to his hands and feet always left ice cold extremities. His ability to walk was almost defunct and it was decided to get a powered wheelchair. Philip knew with each new symptom and each new aid that was required meant he was further away from recovering. For the first time in his life he had a flu jab, not strong enough to endure the severity of a virus. There was no cure, no operation you just had to do the best you could. Philip was far more fortunate than many others and drew on this for some comfort. He intended to be present at the annual 'giving of the tree'.

The Hawthorns had made this gesture for several generations and would continue to do so.

Elizabeth started at Braxby University. It was close enough for her to travel to and from on a daily basis but she elected to stay and share a flat with three other students. Determined to pay her own way the feisty young lady also took on a part-time job. Elizabeth received a call from Thomas saying that he was ok and still travelling. He did not ask for anyone. She relayed the message to her mother and father. They did not mind that he didn't ask after them, grateful that he was Ok.

Chapter 11

Saturday, December 9, 2006

Elizabeth came home for 'the giving of the tree' with two of her friends. Michael and Jasmine, Scarlett would arrive later. The young lady confided in Robert, much to his distress. He really did not want to know about her private life and told her as much.

Elizabeth teased him, "Robert, you are such a prude. You know Scarlett has a thing for you."

Robert answered, "Yes and while we are on that subject could you ask her to please stop with the suggestive talk."

Elizabeth replied, "I can try but when she gets her

teeth into something she will not let go. Take it from me, I know from experience."grinning from ear to ear she added, "Would you like to see her teeth marks?"

Robert uttered, "For God's sake."

The day had turned into a crisp and cold evening, evidenced by the number of people wearing an ensemble of hats, gloves, coats and scarves. Children in pushchairs, eyes only visible through a mountain of blankets and wraps. This year's colour, red. Red fleeces, red bobbles, red fur, red check all set to rosy red cheeks. Robert had attended the previous year's 'the giving of the tree' but did not recall the amount of people to equal this evening's gathering.

It seemed to Robert that the whole village had made an extra effort. He asked the man standing next to him why there was such a big crowd?

The bespectacled red nose replied, "I can't tell you for sure but I can tell you why I'm here. Lord Hawthorn has done an awful lot for the people of this village and now that he has the misfortune of ill health I for one would just like to show my support."

Robert could not help but be touched by the expressed sentiment. Wherever Philip went in life he was preceded by his goodwill to all men and women. Not something he had to work at it was just part and parcel of the man. Even the short time they had been here this evening a number of the village folk had made a point, from genuine concern of wishing Philip well. Philip made a short speech from his wheelchair thanking the entire village for the turnout and it's continued endeavours toward making this a place for all to be welcomed. 'The giving of the tree' had always been a pleasure and would continue to be so. He then turned the tree lights on.

Santa Claus turned up on a sleigh pulled by a lorry and handed out gifts to the village children.

Various stalls up and down the street sold a variety of foodstuffs: hot soup, chestnuts, cheese and assorted pickled vegetables. Not forgetting Mrs Brigsby's pies.

The pub doors were open and people spilled out onto the pavement. Robert stood with Victoria and Philip watching the village enjoy itself. Victoria said to Robert, "Philip is feeling the cold so we will have to depart soon, is that okay with you?" Robert responded, "That will be fine."

At the far end of the village, the War Memorial stood alone and upright. A reminder to anyone entering the village of the chiselled names of men who would never be forgotten. The Memorial had another use, it split the road in two. Dividing and slowing the traffic, tonight the memorial would stand firm against danger, as once the names it proudly displayed had. All of the stalls and activities were at the lower end of the village. Leaving a clear view of Church End where St Matthews shepherded its weekly flock through tree lined pathways and ancient head stones. To the right of St Matthews, Gosling Lane climbed steadily out of the village. It was along this lane that Robert noticed headlights glowing in the dark. Too high for a car or van the vehicle could only be a lorry. Robert thought to himself, what the hell is a lorry doing on country roads at this time of night. The lorry veered into the hedgerow before righting itself back on to the road, a direct line to the village war memorial. Robert started to run, making his way through the crowded street he picked up speed after the last of the stalls. The customary street lights along with the Christmas decorations afforded Robert a good view into the lorry cab. He could see the top of the driver's head slumped over the dashboard, arms hanging loosely by his sides. Robert was at the Memorial the lorry 250 yards away and picking up speed, he sprinted to the left of the Memorial intending to open the driver's door. Now from his side vantage he could see it was a fuel container. Every person in the village stopped what they were doing and looked towards Church End and the impending collision. Transfixed by the unfolding drama as if adhered to the ground, silenced not wanting to distract the performer.

110 yards from the Memorial Robert reached the lorry, he grabbed the handle on the side of the cab and pulled himself up onto the footplate. Leaning backwards he opened the door, 60 yards from the Memorial. Using all his strength he pushed the driver onto the passenger seat and climbed in. The lorry was almost on the Memorial, he swerved to the right, the body of the lorry hit the railings surrounding the Memorial gouging a hole in the metal. The wagon bounced into a metal post, there to protect pedestrians, tearing at the engine. The forward momentum of the truck severely disrupted, Robert guided it to a standstill. He lifted the driver out of the truck and laid him on the pavement. A large group of people came to assist, the driver still breathing and an ambulance was called for.

One of the men in the group who had come to help tapped Robert on the shoulder and said to him, "There are flames coming from beneath the lorry."

Robert looked behind him to see fuel from the engine splashing onto the road and somewhere in the engine he could see fire. He jumped back into the lorry and prayed to God that it would start and if it did that the engine would not explode. It did start and it did not explode but the steering was badly impaired. He knew that a few hundred yards out of the village there were fields lying fallow, getting there proved to be a monumental exercise. The power steering out of action, the offside front wheel buckled in the collision with the metal post combined to create a fairground ride. It was any thing but, the lorry lurching from side to side throwing fuel out of the gaping hole ripped in the side of the tank. Robert managed to coax the truck to go faster. When he looked in the wing mirror flames could be seen licking along and upwards towards the descending fuel. 50 yards to the right turning, which would take him out of the village and into the country. The disused fields just another 400 yards on the left, clear of houses and buildings. The people in the village watched on, astounded as the lorry turned the corner. Flames shooting upwards almost igniting the fuel. Victoria gripped Philips wheelchair so tight she began to shake. Certain that she would not see Robert again. Regretting the missed chances of being with him, holding him and being held by him. Why was he doing this? For people he did not even know. She could not fathom him, throwing his life away when she could have made it all worthwhile. Did he not know?

Robert was clear of the buildings and houses and alongside the fields, he just needed an entrance. Up ahead he could make out a gate, there would be no time to stop and unlock. If the lorry was up to it he would crash through into the field. He picked up speed hoping the impetus would carry him the short distance he needed to go. The wooden gate cracked and splintered from the impact. In the field he lost all control of the steering, he jumped out the door and sprinted to the wall that surrounded the field. Just as he leapt over the wall the lorry exploded sending a ball of flames high into the sky.

Robert took cover behind the wall crouching down to avoid any shards of flying metal. In the village they witnessed the explosion and feared the worst. Victoria numb from shock unable to shed a tear stood rooted to the spot. Elizabeth came to her, putting her arms around her mother whispered in her ear, "I know mother."

An ambulance arrived and tended to the stricken driver, the paramedics informed the gathering crowd that a fire engine was on its way and one of them would stay behind to help with any casualties from the explosion.

Robert confident that there was no more flying debris, walked away from the wall, studied the gap where a gate once stood, the burning lorry gave out an intense heat. Small ashes fluttered down, falling on to Robert as he made his way along the road. He was met by the fire engine, alarm ringing and lights flashing, the big red vehicle came to a halt in front of the former soldier, the paramedic climbed down and wanted to examine him, Robert told him, "If you want to examine me you can do it on the hoof, how is the driver?"

He set a fast pace and was back in the village within 10 minutes. On turning the corner he was greeted by a silent crowd they stared at him as if he were an apparition. Robert walked through the crowd nodding and smiling he could not quite figure out what the problem was he kept going until he came to Victoria and Philip.

Robert said to the Hawthorns, "It is about time we got going, you must be quite cold Philip."

Victoria blurted, "We thought you were dead."

Robert calmly replied, "No, I'm not dead."

He pushed Philip's wheelchair back to the Range

Rover and helped the older man into the car.

"You are quite stiff." commented Robert.

Philip replied, "Yes, the cold does that. I will be ok once I am warmed up."

Directing his question to Victoria Robert asked, "Are Elizabeth and her friends ok for a lift?"

Victoria, "They are getting a taxi later on, to the next town, apparently there is an all-night nightclub."

Philip asked Robert to direct the heat towards his feet. Which gave him some relief but when they transferred from the car to the house he stiffened up again. Although it was still early Philip said he would like to go to bed.

Robert manoeuvred the wheelchair up the stairs with Philip sitting in it. Victoria prepared the bed for her husband and when he was comfortable she went downstairs and joined Robert in the kitchen. He was drinking tea and had made a coffee for Victoria. She sat opposite him and asked if he had seen Alan and Josie?

"Yes" he replied, "they are quite the happy couple."

"Mmmm, love can be found anywhere at any time." she agreed.

The kitchen was silent, outside the yard lights sparkled on the surface of the frost that was forming on anything exposed. Robert could feel Victoria looking at him. Waiting to say something. Eventually she uttered, "Why do you do it?"

Robert had the good sense not to play dumb and ask her 'do what. Victoria was like Sandra in as much they were both very strong characters and would only take so much crap before they demanded straightforward talking.

"It's not something I plan" he began, "if I see a situation developing I try to do something about it before it's too late. My mum told me when I was a kid I was always first to help, any one, any circumstances I would always help" Robert ended hoping that would suffice.

Not happy, Victoria responded, "But why you, there were dozens of men around why could one of them not have done what you did?"

Undeterred Robert retorted, "I do not know, you will

have to ask them."

Victoria glared at Robert. She stood up and went round to Robert's side of the table. Bending down she took his face in her hands and kissed him full on the mouth. Standing upright she whispered,

"The next time you put your life on the line at least I will have that to remember you by."

Chapter 12

The school play started on the 12th of December. Robert had organised the stage used in the village hall could be transferred to the Great Hall.

Children from The Oak Tree School put on a very creditable Jack and the Beanstalk. Elizabeth and Scarlett helped Victoria manage the four continuous nights.

Jenny was in the play and her mother, Jeanette, came along on the Friday evening to watch. Robert spoke to her at length, he really did like her, an uncomplicated lady who had lost her husband several years previously. Doing her best to bring up her daughter by herself and by the looks of it doing a good job. She had met someone but as yet had not introduced Jenny to him. She had also witnessed his heroics at 'the giving of the tree'. A regular action man was how she described him. When the performance was over he said goodbye to her but part of him wished hat he were the man to be introduced to Jenny.

Robert stood outside for a while and let the cold air bring him back to this senses. A voice called him it was Victoria.

"Are you okay?" She asked him.

"I am fine, just thinking." he replied.

"I seen you talking to Jeanette, you like her?"

Robert considered the impossible situation he was in and the beautiful woman standing next to him.

"Yes I do like her but that is not what I am thinking of" he continued, "strange as it may sound I miss having my family with me."

Victoria new Robert would be by himself at Christmas so she asked him again, "You are more than welcome to come to Scotland with us. Christmas is no time to be by yourself."

Robert responded, "Thank you, but no thanks."

He was sorely tempted, it was Victoria he wanted to be with. After all, he had been by himself before and in much more dangerous conditions. No need to start feeling sorry for himself and playing little boy lost.

25th December 2006

On Christmas Day morning Robert spoke with Luke and Sandra who were at Sandra's parents for Christmas.

Robert went up to the house and checked that all was safe and secure. One of the farm hands just finishing for the day spoke with Robert for a few moments but was in a rush to get away. To spend the day with his family.

Late afternoon he called his sister in New York, she was preparing to enjoy a very traditional Christmas Day, turkey stuffing the whole works. It was snowing there and her family had gone out sledging.

Because of the time delay he sent his brother in Australia an e-mail wishing him all the very best and would speak to him in the New Year.

Early evening Victoria called him said that she missed his company and was looking forward to seeing him in the New Year. The phone call left him feeling lonelier than ever.

Christmas 2006 was a very isolated experience for Robert. Over the years he had spent many a long hour by himself but this was different. Much to his eternal shame he realised that above all else he was pining for Victoria. Not his brother and sister thousands of miles away not even the camaraderie he felt in the army. Thoughts of Philip's health came into his head at which stage he decided to go for a run. He combined the run with checking the house one more time and the various barns dotted around. Afterwards he did feel better the exercise had done him good.

28th December 2006

Robert received a call from Victoria saying that Philip had an idea in his head to go skiing. Neither she, nor his family could deter him.

29th December 2006

Victoria called again. Philip was determined to go

skiing and was wondering if Luke would like to go?

Robert told her that Sandra, Luke and friends were already going skiing to the Lecht region in Scotland.

Victoria hesitated for a moment before saying, "You will come, say you will Robert?"

Robert had mistakenly understood that he was already going, he replied, "Of course I will go, why do you need the reassurance?"

"I just do." Victoria said in response.

The Hawthorns returned on the 3rd January 2007. Robert was at the house waiting for them, Victoria was not her usual calm self. As soon as she could she took Robert to one side and said, "I greatly appreciate you coming skiing with us but I would much prefer that you would try and talk Philip out of it. He is under the illusion that the cold clear air will benefit him. When we all know the effect the cold has on him."

Robert did not need to seek Philip out, he came to Robert and said, "I know you have been asked to speak with me, forget it. I am going and that's that."

On Christmas Day Alan asked Josie to marry him. They declined the invite to go skiing with Philip and Victoria, instead they would use the time to prepare for their wedding, February 14th 2007.

Philip, Victoria, Elizabeth, Scarlett and Robert set off on the 10th of January 2007. The group that departed returned a very different thinking collection of people.

Author's Biography

Jack Jones lives in Bedfordshire. He has Multiple Sclerosis and discovered writing after a letter was published in an MS magazine about a trip he took, it was a letter of hope and optimism which the Editors felt was worthy of publication. Gabriel finds writing a release for his creative mind and a focus for the future.

This is his first published novel.

Lightning Source UK Ltd.
Milton Keynes UK
UKOW051215211111

182424UK00001B/29/P

9 781438 935362